Shotgun

It was a mess. There was a stack of bullet-riddled bodies, the sheriff was out of action, forty grand was missing and nobody knew the what, where or whom.

Shotgun rider Brill Williams was no lawman, but with his best pal killed and the sheriff down after taking a bullet, he'd sure as hell make it his business to take up the hunt. Snag was, he was no man-tracker either and all his leads were drawing blanks.

But then, with nothing left to go on, his attention turns to the former bank teller. Could she be the missing step in his quest for bloody retribution.

Shotgun

B. J. Holmes

A Black Horse Western

ROBERT HALE · LONDON

ISBN 0 7090 7677 0

Robert Hale Limited
Clerkenwell House
Clerkenwell Green
London EC1R 0HT

*For Bob, film-maker and life-long friend,
who was there at the beginning of the fantasising*

Typeset by
Derek Doyle & Associates, Liverpool.
Printed and bound in Great Britain by
Antony Rowe Limited, Wiltshire

ONE

Natty Williams inhaled deeply of the manliness against her nostrils. Moving up behind her husband, she had put her arms around his naked torso and snuggled her head into the flesh between his shoulder blades. 'I do wish you'd get another job, Brill.'

'Hold your horses,' honey,' he said, pausing in his shaving to examine the blade and his chin in turn. 'I nearly sliced a chunk out of my good looks then.' Satisfied there was no damage he continued scraping. 'Hey, how's a guy supposed to get ready for work when he's got a darn limpet stuck to him?'

'There you go again, Brill Williams, changing the subject.'

He shaved the remaining lather from his face and put the razor on one side. He wiped his face and assessed the result in the mirror, before turning round to his wife. He gripped her shoulders and held her at arm's length. 'I know the money ain't any great shakes, honey, but at least I bring home more than if I was cow-punching or working in some store.'

'It's not the money, you know that,' she said, pulling him to her. 'Every day I worry from the moment you leave the door till the moment you come back.'

'And I keep telling you there's nothing to worry about. I've been riding shotgun on the stage for years and nothing's happened yet. And not likely to.'

'There's got to be *some* risk or the company wouldn't require an armed guard. Where there's guns, someday they'll be used.'

He extricated himself from her embrace, rinsed his razor and brush and placed them on the shelf. 'I've told you before. Having somebody riding shotgun is for show. It's easy money. The company has the contract for the US Mail and it's a requirement of the contract that there is a guard. On the other hand, only the seventh son of a jackass would try to steal the mail because interfering with the mail would bring a posse of US marshals after the perpetrators.'

'The world is full of jackasses.'

He pulled on his shirt. 'How many stage-men go out each morning in an ironed shirt with razor sharp creases to prove it? I'm truly blessed.'

'Yes, blessed with one of those jackasses you mentioned – me, a woman fool enough to let her husband expose himself to danger on a daily basis.'

He shook his head as he reached for his jacket. 'I don't know. A guy marries a gal and all she wants to do is change him.'

She patted her slightly distended stomach. 'When this little fellow is born, I don't want him growing up fatherless.'

'Fellow? What is this? I told you I'd ordered a girl.'

He pulled on his coat and kissed her forehead. 'OK, honey, I'll strike a bargain. First time there's any trouble, I'll start looking for another line of work. Fair enough?'

'Then it might be too late.'

He donned his hat and took the Sharps gun from the pegs on the wall. At .50 calibre it was a cumbersome weapon designed for buffalo hunting. But the sheer size of it made it a deterrent, he reckoned, although he'd never triggered its deafening boom in anger.

'Honey, I never knowed anybody who fretted as much as you,' he said, giving her one more kiss. 'But you know what? I wouldn't change my little darling for the world.'

He stepped out into the bright early sunlight

and walked along the rutted track that consti-tuted Lauderburg's main street. Over at the stage depot, the driver was checking the thorough-braces in preparation for the first trip of the day.

'Howdy, Florida,' Brill greeted.

The oldster looked up. A droop moustache, rampantly out of control, pure white save for brown juice stains in the middle, covered the lower part of his face so that neither the lips form-ing 'Morning, Brill,' nor the welcoming grin accompanying the greeting could be seen.

'Get some coffee going, younker,' he said, 'and I'll be with you in a shake.' And he moved to inspecting the wheel rims.

'How many years have I been telling you, you don't have to do that?' Brill chided in mock repri-mand. Even though maintenance was the respon-sibility of others, Florida Jones was of the old school and gave his vehicle a good check-over every morning.

'Yeah, you shave-tailed whipper-snapper. And how many times have I told you: you want a good job doing, you do it yourself?'

James Goodman came to the bottom of the column of figures, made a note of the total with his pencil, then grunted noisily. 'I've added up these wretched things three times and got three different answers.'

He slammed his pencil down on his desk. 'Mrs Scarpelli. Can you come and work out this total? I'll tend counter.'

'Certainly, Mr Goodman,' came the voice from the front room of the bank. Seconds later his teller appeared at the door of his office.

And once again he wondered what he had done to deserve such an employee. Her cheeks blushed with rosy health, her lips bore the freshest of smiles, her eyes sparkled with good humour. But, more than a heart-stopping appearance, she embodied accomplishments in her lettering and figuring far beyond that which could be expected from the usual run of frontier female.

He pointed to the frustrating document on his desk. 'If you will, Mrs Scarpelli. See what you can make of these amounts.'

She sat down and set about her task while he took her place in the front. Just after he had tended to a customer, Mrs Scarpelli appeared beside him and placed the paper before him. There was a circle round one of his figures. 'Your second total was right. I've checked it twice.'

He shook his head. 'Then I know it's right. I don't know what I would do without you. As I have said many times, you are most worthy of your position. Nothing is to be found wanting. Your industry and proficiency constantly endear you to me.'

She smiled. 'That's very kind of you, Mr Goodman. Now, if you'll excuse me we have another customer waiting.'

The bank's business continued in an unrushed way for another hour. Then, just before lunchtime, a man presented himself before the counter.

He was an imposing figure in buckskins and Hessian boots, with a broad neckcloth and apple green coat with steel buttons almost as large as dollar pieces. He took off his expensive flat, wide-brimmed hat and laid it on the counter.

'Morning, ma'am.'

There was something soft about the accent. He opened his jacket, exposing a dark red vest, and he withdrew a document from an inner pocket. 'I'd be obliged if you could please cash this bank draft.'

She took it from him and scrutinized it. 'Fifty dollars?' she observed with a nod. She looked up and carefully took in his appearance. 'Fine,' she continued, 'but it's company policy that such documents should be cleared by the manager. Just a formality, you understand?'

'Of course.'

The man looked around the room as she moved to the back. Shortly, Goodman appeared, holding the document. 'You have some identifi-cation, Mr Pearce?'

'Certainly.' The man took some letters and other documents from his pocket and slipped them under the grille.

Goodman inspected them. 'Everything seems to be in order,' he said, returning the papers. 'Go ahead, Mrs Scarpelli.'

'Our discount is five per cent,' she said, resuming charge of the transaction. The man nodded.

'A reasonable charge.'

'And how would you like it?'

'As it comes.'

She opened the drawer and counted the money. 'There you are, Mr Pearce. Forty-seven dollars and fifty cents.'

'Pleasure doing business with you, ma'am.'

He put away the money, and donned his hat. He touched the rim and, with a smile, departed.

She watched him disappear through the door and then looked up at the clock. 'Mr Goodman, do you mind if I take an early lunch break? I have some shopping to do.'

'Of course, my dear. Take your time.'

In the back room he watched her gather her things. 'Is your husband still working away?' he asked.

'Yes.'

'I can't understand why he doesn't arrange for employment locally, with such a lady at home and all.'

She let the compliment pass, checked the set of her bonnet on her head and stepped into the counter office. As she made her way out, the front door was opened by the mailman.

'Good day, Mrs Scarpelli,' he said, touching his hat and stepping aside to allow her to pass. She nodded in reciprocation as she exited.

The man closed the door and walked over to the bar-fronted counter. 'Got some late mail, Mr Goodman,' he said, pushing some envelopes under the bars. 'I was passing this way so I thought I'd drop it in.'

'Much obliged, Bert,' the bank manager said. They exchanged a few pleasantries before the mailman carried on his way.

Goodman used a paperknife to slit open the envelopes. He cast an eye over the correspondence then turned his attention to the last item, a firm little package. It contained a letter and a key. He nodded in understanding as his eyes skimmed the letter. He slipped the key into his vest pocket and took the documents into his office.

Out on the boardwalk, Mrs Scarpelli was now a block away, looking up and down the street. Finally she espied her last customer settling into a seat outside the stage depot.

She proceeded along the street, eventually taking occupancy in the vacant seat beside him.

'Leaving town, Mr Pearce?' she said, without looking at him. He turned to appraise the speaker.

'Please don't look my way, or give any indication that we are talking,' she continued.

'I don't understand,' he said, facing the street.

'Let me make myself plain. Should you attempt to leave town until we have had some discussion, I will notify the town's law agency that at 11.45 this morning you successfully defrauded the bank by presenting a forged bank draft.'

'Forged bank draft?

'Please don't treat me as an imbecile, Mr Pearce. We have the evidence under lock and key. A good forgery, I will grant you that, but nevertheless a sham document.'

'Fake? It was vetted by the manager himself.'

'Mr Goodman is a kindly soul but how he got into banking, I don't know. He can't tell the difference between a debit and a credit. And it is the same incompetence that prevents him from recognizing a forgery when it is presented to him. Rest assured, Mr Pearce, it would take less than a minute in a court of law for someone with a trained eye to confirm its fraudulence. Incidentally, I told an untruth back there in the bank: I have sufficient authority to handle drafts. The bank has no policy that they should be checked by the manager. Not that the procedure would provide any safeguard with the present incumbent.'

'Then why—'

'I brought Mr Goodman to the counter in order that he might *see* you,' she interrupted. 'He doesn't know it, but I was using him as a witness, should the need arise.'

The man coughed. 'Should the need arise? I still fail to see where this conversation is going.'

'To begin with, the confidence you displayed when presenting the forgery at the bank tells me you are no beginner in these matters. That interests me.'

'In what matters?'

'Please do not play games with me, Mr Pearce. I will call you Mr Pearce, although I doubt that that is your real name.'

'OK, Mrs What-ever-your-name-is, if you see me as some criminal, why don't you inform the authorities right now?'

'You will use the forty-seven dollars and fifty cents that you fraudently took from the bank to book into a hotel. Then, this evening you will call at my home. My husband is away so we shall not be disturbed.'

He cleared his throat again. 'What's this all about?'

She ignored the question and described the location of her dwelling. 'Be there prompt at eight. And, in your coming, ensure you are not seen.'

He took a watch from his vest. 'The stage is due shortly. Before I make any commitment I still want to know what this is about.'

'A discussion is all I require. If our exchange does not come to some conclusion, you may catch your stage tomorrow. For the cost of a mere night's lodging – from your ill-gotten gains, I might add – you may leave without charges being brought against you and be on your way unimpeded. Do we have an arrangement?'

'OK, lady, I'll go through with this crazy thing. Not because I'm guilty but simply because I'm intrigued.'

'Very well. By the way, do not consider taking advantage of my being a mere woman. By the time you come tonight a sealed document will have been lodged in a security box – whether at the bank or with an attorney, I am not divulging. It will contain the charge of bank fraud, explaining how you presented a forged document for encashment. It will describe you in great detail, together with your manner of speaking which is that of a Canadian. And, of course, it will explain how Mr Goodman also saw you and could possibly add to the description. The envelope will be sealed with the inscription that it is only to be opened in the event of anything happening to me.'

'You think of everything.'

She smiled and nodded. 'Mr Goodman says that often about me.' Then, she rose. 'Till eight.' And she left without giving him a glance.

TWO

The house was where she'd said it was. It looked unoccupied as he approached, but closer he detected the faint glow from some turned-down lamp. He knocked the door. Heard footsteps on boards, then the door opened.

'Pearce,' he said.

'Yes, I know. I saw you from the window. Come in.'

Inside she closed the curtains and turned up the lamps. 'Sit down,' she said, pointing to a settee before the embers of a fire. 'Whiskey?'

'Fine, ma'am.'

He noticed her auburn hair, previously pinned in a bun, now cascading over her shoulders. She opened a cabinet revealing an array of spirits. 'What kind?'

'Scotch.'

'What kind of Scotch?'

He leant back with his arm draped over the back of the settee, and appraised the selection. 'A dash of that malt, ma'am, would do fine. With a splash of water.'

'Ah, a man of taste.'

She attended to his drink and poured a bourbon for herself. As she crossed the room to join him on the settee, he rose, accepted the glass and allowed her to sit before resuming his seat.

'Your health, ma'am,' he said, raising his glass. Then, after a sip, 'This is sure classy stuff.'

He glanced around at the plush surroundings, then back at the array of expensive bottles. He thought of her behind the bank teller's grille with her pinned-up hair; the schoolmarmish voice; her prim and proper manner. And concluded there was a mite more to this woman than first appeared.

'To business,' she said. 'Now, Mr Pearce, you know what I do for a living. What do you do?'

'No specific trade. A bit here, a bit there.'

'I don't like your answer. You're being evasive. Let's start with the fake bank draft. How did you come by that?'

'I accepted it in good faith. I didn't know it was a fake. In fact, come to think of it, I only have your word that it is a fake.'

She sipped her drink and looked into his eyes. 'It's a fake all right. And you're still being evasive.'

18

She looked closer. 'And lying, too.'

He felt uncomfortable under the scrutiny. What was this woman? One of those vaudeville mind-readers?

'You're tense,' she said, relaxing back. 'Let me put you at your ease. The account of today's fraud is under wraps. And, if this evening turns out satisfactorily, it will remain so. At the same time, anything you tell me tonight will remain within these walls. Now, you are a criminal by career, that is plain. The confidence you displayed when you presented the forgery at the bank indicates you are well practised in deceit and that you can handle people. A criminal, yes, but not an ordinary criminal. You have the style and manner of a gentleman. Veritable qualities but, maybe more important, I sense that you have brains. And that interests me.'

She smiled at his silence. 'To proceed, you tell me you came by the fake draft innocently. However, I suspect that that valise up in your hotel room is full of them. Now, the truth, Mr Pearce. As I promised, it will go no further.'

He looked around the room, then back at the woman. 'I have to tell you, Mrs Scarpelli, there is something odd about all this. Here we are, two strangers, having a drink, then you start asking weird questions. How do I know this isn't some kind of set-up? Your old man could be the law and

19

this whole thing has been rigged for me to cough up to something.'

'This is not a sophisticated metropolis, Mr Pearce. We only have one lawman in town, Sheriff Mosely.' She laughed dismissively. 'And as far as Frank is concerned, he's as crooked as I suspect you are.'

'In what way?'

'That is for later. First, a little more about you.'

'OK, what do you want to know?'

'Well, let's be specific. Have you ever used a gun in your line of work?'

He shrugged. 'Occasionally.'

'Banks?'

'Once.'

She poured him another drink. 'And what other businesses have you relieved of their resources?'

'Specialized in mining and lumber payrolls.'

'Was that alone or in a gang?'

'Always used others. Safety in numbers.'

'Used – that means you were the boss.'

'Yeah.'

'A regular gang?'

'No. I would pull a gang together whenever I needed it. In my business I have a lot of contacts.'

'So you can handle men,' she said, as she studied him. 'And that was back in Canada.'

Jeez, he thought, she was a mind-reader. 'Yeah,

how'd you know?' he asked.

'Mining, lumber, your Canadian accent. Not a difficult guess.' After a pause, she added. 'I was right. You *are* Canadian, aren't you?'

'By adoption, yes, you might say. But I was born in the old USA – leastways it's American soil now – in a little town you'll never have heard of. Place called Nome.'

'You're right, I've never heard of it.'

'At the end of the world, out on the Seward Peninsula.'

'I'm still no wiser.'

'Alaska, ma'am. A place that God did not design for the habitation of man or beast. It's locked in by mountains on the east and you can only really get to it on the seaward side by the Bering Strait. But the Strait freezes over for six months in the year, during which time nobody can get in or out.' He chuckled. 'Well, I got *out* as soon as I could. Spent most of my time in Canada. Which is how come I picked up their way of talking. They got a big country up there but you name it, I've worked it: Vancouver, Winnipeg, Montreal.'

'Doing what?'

'Relieving folks who'd got too much cash of their loose change. I'm sure you can guess how, and I use the term "loose change" euphemistically. But, I have to say, Nome has been good to me. I've pulled some big jobs and whenever the Mounties were looking for me I'd catch the last boat up at the end of summer and visit my kin for a spell. The redcoats had no idea where I was at and even if they did, they couldn't get at me. Huh, they're supposed to always get their man – but you're looking at one man they never got their fur gloves on.'

He sipped his drink. 'Every region has got its haven for owl-hoots. Down here you've got Tucson, El Paso, the Badlands.'

'So what brought you south?'

'Change of climate, see more of the world. You don't know what cold is till you've lived up near the Arctic Circle, ma'am, with nothing but inbreeds, muskox and mush-dogs for company. Besides there's been rich pickings down here too. Then I found that if a guy dressed up, spun a yarn he could get money out of folk without using a gun. I figure if you've got what it takes you can pull a good dollar anywhere.'

'You ever done time?'

'No.'

She replenished the glasses but instead of returning to the settee, she headed for the stairs. At the foot she turned and whispered, 'If you want your next drink you'll have to come and get it.'

He watched her disappear upstairs. Nonplussed, he listened to the creaking of the floorboards above his head. Hell, what was this?

Eventually, after a long silence, curiosity got the better of him and he ventured slowly up the stairs.

He couldn't believe his eyes when he located her room. She was lying naked on a large double bed. 'You took your time,' she murmured, patting the bed beside her. As he sat in the indicated place, she began pulling at his clothes.

Seconds later, she was sitting astride him, dangling her full breasts in his face.

He lay beside her, totally spent. He lit a cigarette and surveyed the vision before him. It was hard to imagine that the fiery tigress that had bitten at his flesh and drained his body to the point of exhaustion had earlier that day been the lady bank clerk with pinned-up hair, bonnet and a skirt that trailed the ground.

'Is that what this was all about?' he asked. 'Getting me into bed?'

'What would you say, if I said yes?'

'I'd have said you only had to ask, ma'am. You're a mighty attractive woman and I'm an obliging sort of feller. What's the problem? Your old man can't give you what you want?'

She ignored the questions. 'A woman can tell a lot about a man's character by the way he is in bed.'

'And what have you learned?'

'I think I've learned enough.'

'Enough for what?'

'Let's go downstairs. We've got some talking to do.'

Still puzzled, he shrugged. 'You're the hostess.'

He dropped his head back, and immediately grunted. His head had hit something hard under the pillow. He reached beneath and withdrew a derringer. Short-barrelled, small calibre, not the best of weapons for a shooting contest, but could be deadly within a range of six feet. He twirled the gun on his finger, let it slap back into position and sighted it at some imaginary target on the ceiling. 'You know, ma'am, a guy can tell a lot about a woman by the equipment she totes in bed.'

They were dressed again and downstairs.

'This conversation has got a mite one-sided,' he said. 'You know a heck about me, what about you?'

She drew her housecoat about her and brushed away fluff. 'My family were quite well-to-do. Sent me to finishing school. Provided me with enough skills to become a clerk. Not the best of occupations but at least, I didn't have to earn a pittance in the drudgery of domestic service like many girls of my age. Then I met Frank; I was young and I fell in love. My family resisted at first because he was without social polish or background. However he did have money and that rendered him acceptable to them. Yes, he was a rough diamond. So, we married. Then Pa died and left me enough to buy this place.

'Anyway, in time, things cooled off between us, but at least I was living comfortably, as you can see. And matters continued in that way until I began to learn more about what kind of man Frank was. He was a rough diamond all right, but more rough than diamond. The fact was, he was nothing but a small stakes thief. It had just happened that, when I first met him, he had recently been part of what in his circle they call a heist which had landed him with a big haul. Enough to give him the veneer of being of independent means and not needing to work. But I was to learn it had merely been a lucky job. He'd never known so much money in his life. And in time he blew it. In reality he was a penny ante thief and has never been part of a big job since.'

'Where is he now?'

She chuckled humourlessly. 'Just finishing time for trying to knock over a dry goods store. A dry goods store, I ask you. And the bozo couldn't even pull that off. At least it was an out-of-county job so townsfolk don't know of his circumstances.' She looked around the room. 'So, Mr Pearce, I am in a bind without even Frank's pittance. I've had to borrow against the house and cash is fast running out, so it won't be long before I have to give up the place all together. My income from the bank is not enough to keep me in the style to which I am accustomed and Frank is now more a millstone than an asset.'

'When does Frank get released?'

'In two days. So, given a day's travelling he'll be back that night or the next day.'

'And where do I come in?'

She poured more drinks and sat beside him. 'I think I've got your measure and you can handle what I've got in mind.'

'Which is?'

'How long have you been in town?'

'Couple of days.'

'Then you may be aware of the mine just out of town.'

' I saw it when I came in.'

'Well, some time back the workers came to the end of the lode. The company spent a lot of money opening up new tunnels and excavations but couldn't find another vein. When, a month or so back, it became clear the site was exhausted, the company collapsed. Our bank not only handled the company money but held most of the miners' accounts. To use the vernacular, all hell broke loose and there was a run on the bank. Within hours the cash ran out and Mr Goodman had to put up an early closing sign. That made things worse.'

She shook her head and smiled at the recollection. 'There was a queue along the length of Main Street. However, what folk didn't realize is, one reason he'd put up the sign was to give himself time to negotiate with the other banks in town. Although they are competitors, there is some camaraderie amongst the banking fraternity. A temporary agreement was struck whereby they agreed to lend cash; so within a couple of hours we'd opened again and customers could withdraw their money. Many of the folk immediately opened up new accounts with the other banks. So for the rest of the day, money was going out of our door, into other banks; then runners would bring bags of it back to our establishment via the back door.'

He shook his head. 'Crazy.'

'Not crazy,' she said. 'It's the way the system works. Ordinary folks are under the illusion that banking is based on money. It's not. No bank in the world could withstand a demand for cash to be withdrawn from all deposits. The resources are there, but not in cash. Their assets are largely made up of pieces of paper, certificates, bonds. All banking, whether it's Wall Street or Hicksville USA, is based on confidence. As long as there's confidence the system works.

'Goodman had organized a regular supply of hard cash. As a result, by the next day folks had realized that they could withdraw their money from our bank at will. So they stopped withdrawing and the system settled down again.'

'As easy as that?'

'Not quite that easy. Although the other banks in town had agreed to bale us out, it was only on a temporary basis. They are in competition, after all. We needed eventually to pay them back, while at the same time restoring our own liquidity. That could only be achieved by head office in Denver sending out hard cash.'

'And?'

'That is scheduled to arrive on the stage on Friday. There will be more hard cash on that coach than the line has ever carried before. Or ever will again.'

'I think I'm beginning to see.'

'I sincerely hope so. Otherwise I have wrongly credited you with brains, Mr Pearce.'

He raised his glass. 'Please, call me Ellis.'

'Ellis Pearce.' She savoured the name. 'It has a ring.'

'And you are? We've been to bed and I still don't know your given name.'

'You call me Mrs Scarpelli, Mr Pearce.'

'OK, Mrs Scarpelli, let's stop beating about the bush. Be specific.'

28

'I'm proposing, Mr Pearce, that you and I organize an operation to take the money.'

'And how much are we talking about?'

'We are talking about forty thousand US dollars, Mr Pearce.'

He whistled.

THREE

It was developing into a long night. With another drink, he lit a cigarette and leant an arm along the back of the settee. 'OK, tell me more.'

'It'll be coming in from Denver. That's the north trail into town. I can give you the scheduled times but you'll have to reconnoitre to pick the best spot.'

'Why do we have to have a go at the stage? Seems to me it would be a mite easier to pull off the job when the money's here in the bank. There's no guard as far as I can see and only you and Goodman on the premises, I presume.'

'That is so but several reasons militate against that option. Firstly, Sheriff Mosely, I mentioned before. He's a seasoned lawman. Tough man, ex-army. He's usually out on Main Street. The law office is only a few yards down the street on the other side from the bank and he's often on the seat outside. Even if he isn't, he will be in the vicinity. You will have noticed Lauderberg is not very big so that means wherever he is he will be close by. Moreover, he is conscientious about his job and if he is not on the scene, he will certainly take chase very quickly, probably with a posse. You will be at a disadvantage. Moreover, no matter how big the mask you put around your face your voice is very distinctive. Mr Goodman has already seen and heard you, and could probably give a useful description. No, the money has to be taken before the stage gets to town.'

'I'm still not sure that's the way. There's a heap of snags. Fact is, Mrs Scarpelli, nobody ever made a living robbing stage-lines. That's why it's gone out style.'

'Yes, and that's because they typically come away with a haul of thirty dollars and a few paste necklaces. Maybe a five-dollar watch if they're lucky. I've told you this baby is going to be loaded.'

'OK, but small pickings is not the only reason nobody knocks over stages. One of those big-bore jobs that shotgun riders carry can take a guy's head off. Then, if you don't stop the vehicle and they makes a dash for it, you don't know who you can run into along the trail while you're chasing it. You could run smack into the law, trailriders, anybody.'

'That's why the job has to be well-thought out. Now here's what I want you to do . . .'

'Hold your hosses, ma'am,' he interrupted. 'I didn't hear myself saying yes. As far as I'm concerned I've fulfilled my part of the bargain. You said to stay over in town for the night and listen to what you've got to say, is all. I've done that, so if I choose to light out tomorrow, then that's the end of it.'

'The way you've been talking I thought—'

'Well, you thought wrong. I ain't rushing into anything. As far as this operation that you're suggesting goes, I've still gotta check the thing out, see if it's feasible. You're selling it to me like it's a foregone conclusion, but you're a woman and haven't been involved in this kind of work before. Even if you're on the square with me, there still might be something you've overlooked. For a start, knocking off a stage is going to need more than one man and it's too short a notice for me to get any of my pals in.'

'That's why the men involved have to be from town.'

He grimaced. 'I don't care for doing a job with guys I ain't worked with before. Besides, I'm a stranger in town. How can I pull a bunch together quickly? Do you know anybody?'

She laughed. 'I'm a bank clerk, Mr Pearce. I don't move in such circles. No, that's where Frank comes in. He's got nothing between his ears but he knows the town's no-goods. He'll be able to pull in some dependables. Then as long as they're kept in the dark about things and just told what they have to do, they should be usable without any trouble.'

'You know the security arrangements of the stage-line?'

'Yes. The regular stage has never attracted the attention of road agents before and only carries the usual one man riding shotgun.' She smiled. 'And Little Miss Innocent here has been handling all the correspondence with headquarters and knows the thinking. Because it has never been robbed before and nobody knows of its special cargo on that day, the bank arc only sending one guard with the money. He'll be armed of course. Along with the driver, that makes three.'

He pondered on the mechanics. 'So, given the element of surprise, by that reckoning a total of four men should be enough to handle the business. Throw in another for good measure, making five. More would be safer, but we have to balance that against the fact that the fewer who know the better. And, of course, the less to divvy up with afterwards. Say I go along with this, what happens afterwards?'

'You hang on to the money for as long as you can beforc divvying up. The rest of the gang will be local men. Once they've got a few grand in their poke they're likely to come back to town and start spending. They do that and one or two of them might get picked up. The sheriff will know it's a local job and suspicion could come my way. Worse, they could spill the beans as to what they know.'

'With me as the link man, they won't know much.'

'They'll know Frank's in on it. Any of them spills just that much and it'll give a direct link to me. So you delay the divvying-up as long as you can.'

'Then what?'

'We arrange to meet up. Denver is far enough away and big enough to get lost in for a couple of days.'

She eyed him. 'My only problem is – can I trust you? There's a lot of money involved.'

'Your interest in me lies in my being a crook. I'm not denying there's been a poster on me gun-tacked to a tree-stump somewhere before – but I got standards, ma'am. When I make a deal with a man I honour the agreement, just as I expect him to do the same. Likewise, if the "man" is a woman. Now, let's get back to Frank. All I know of him is what you've told me. Can I rely on him to pull in the right guys?'

'The only folk he keeps company with are men

with mean appetites in common. Don't concern yourself. He knows all the local no-goods.'

'OK, but how do I get to know him? Do I meet him here?'

'No. He mustn't know we're connected. In all matters concerning me he's got a touch of the green-eyed monster. Just a hint of another man and there's no saying what he'll do.'

'So how do I get acquainted with him?'

'I can describe him. And you can watch the house. You'll see him coming and going.'

'OK, say I can recognize him. How do we meet up?'

'I'm sure you'll find a way.'

'There's still a problem. We gotta move fast. How do I get him to trust me, a complete stranger, in such a short time?'

'Ever been to Omaha?'

'I've passed through.'

'That'll be enough. One of Frank's close pals is out there. Hal Johnson, otherwise known as the Randado Kid. They've done jobs together. You can say Hal said for you to look him up if ever you're down this way. That'll put you in good with Frank.'

'Ain't the smartest thing, pretending to know a guy. Easy to get tripped up that way.'

'I'll give you what I know about Hal. Enough to get by. I'm sure that, as an experienced grifter, you will be able to stretch a little information and make it sound convincing.'

Ellis nodded, remaining quiet while he pondered on it. Then, 'Won't my knowing what the stage is carrying arouse Frank's suspicions about where I got the information?'

'The bank's headquarters are in Denver. You can say you picked up the information there.'

'No, that won't wash. Frank would know that if I was planning the job from at a distance, I'd bring my own men. Only a greenhorn would lay on a big job such as this using unknown boys. Frank would know that.' He thought on it. 'Does this Goodman get out much in the evening?'

'He has a penchant for playing cards. Plays in the Ocotillo Saloon now and again.'

'Does he drink?'

'Rye.'

'OK, I'll say I was playing cards with him one night and he let it slip when he'd got too much rye down him.'

'Yes, that should do it.'

He lit another cigarette. 'OK, ma'am. I think we might have something going. The next thing I want to do is case the route. From Denver, you say?'

'Yes, on the northern trail from Mortimer. That's the last connection before town.'

FOUR

Next morning he bought a horse and took the northern trail. Along the route his mind logged twists and turns and other natural features. Twenty miles out he reined in. He dismounted with a grimace and worked his shoulders to ease the ache in the small of his back. It had been a long time since he had ridden a horse.

Ahead there were just flats, probably all the way to Mortimer. But it didn't matter. He didn't need to go any further. He had already seen the most likely spot.

He drew rein to rest a while. As he smoked reflectively, he couldn't get the image of the woman out of his thoughts. Her touch, her flesh, her perfume. He stamped out the cigarette and forced his mind back to the business in hand.

He swung round his horse and returned, stopping some ten miles out of town where the trail rose to go through a pass. It was a big cutting through the rocks which dominated the landscape. He dismounted, tethered his horse out of view and worked his way up. From the top he could see the trail in both directions effectively to the horizon; and no habitations in sight.

He was making his descent when he glimpsed a stage heading towards Lauderburg. He pushed his hat back and dipped down behind rocks to ensure he wouldn't be seen, and watched. On the approach to the pass there was a stretch of flat land before the trail hit a steep grade. The driver used the flat to get up speed but the rise was about half a mile long so that before they got to the top, the mules were down to a walking pace. Yes, this would be the strategic place to jump the thing. The mules wouldn't be in a state to make a break for it, no matter how hard the driver whipped them. And near the top there were rocks on either side so the coach couldn't be turned. Ideal.

He returned to town, left the horse at the livery, made a detour on foot round the town and reported back to Mrs Scarpelli via the back door. She smiled as she watched him step into the house. The stiffness in his movement was evidence that absence from the saddle had exerted its toll.

He described the site he had located as being

the most advantageous location for the job.

'That's Big Fir Pass,' she concluded. 'Yes. I do recall it has a steep grade. That would slow the coach. Admirable idea.'

'Still one thing's worrying me. With no one knowing of this special cargo, it isn't going to be long before someone figures it's an inside job. Once they've discounted Goodman and anybody else back at the bank's head office, the process of elimination will point to you. You'll be in a spot.'

'I've worked that out. I have a sick sister out at Mortimer. Or so Mr Goodman thinks. I've had my eye open for an opportunity such as this for a long time and have already made myself scarce twice on the pretext of visiting her. So Shortly I'm going to get an urgent message she's seriously ill – on her deathbed, poor thing – and I'll have to leave quick. Goodman won't suspect anything. At least not at first. By the time he does, I'll be well away.'

'I'm impressed. You've really thought this through.'

'Don't be patronizing. This is make or break for me too.'

'What about the house?'

'No loss. We've had to take so many loans, it's mortgaged up to the hilt.'

'Then what?'

'That's up to you, Ellis.'

'What do you mean?'

'When you came striding into the bank I thought, now there's a striking-looking fellow. Then, when you pulled your brazen little fraud, I merely saw you as a duded-up tinhorn, no more than a possible catspaw in my plan.'

'And now?'

'My original idea was when this was over we meet up and split our share of the proceeds. She paused. 'But we could keep our share intact . . .'

'You mean . . .'

'Yes. I don't see you as merely a handsome pawn any longer. To tell the truth, I've developed feelings for you. I didn't think I would, but there it is. I've not felt like this for a long, long time. You've aroused feelings in me that I thought were long since dead. So . . . we could hitch up together, move on and settle some place. Neither of us is getting any younger. You know they say two can live as cheaply as one. Well, twenty grand is not chicken-feed. It will set us up for life.'

He pulled her to him. 'To tell you the truth, I've been thinking that way myself, but I didn't dare to say.'

She fell against his chest and threw her arms around him. 'Oh, Ellis.'

He took her face in his hands and kissed her passionately. For a while they stood in an embrace. Then he said, 'Once you've left town it's only going to be matter of time before they figure you have a connection with the job.'

'I'll change my name.'

He chuckled.

'What's funny?'

'You're going to change your name; and I don't yet know the name of the woman I'm planning to run away with!'

'Ann,' she said coyly.

'Well, Ann, even with a change of name you still need to get out of the way. Listen, I've got an idea. It's still spring. When we meet up in Denver we can head north to Anchorage and take the boat up to Nome. You remember I told you about the place? We can spend a season there. Tucked out of the way, it'll give us a breather till the heat wears off and give us time to think about our more permanent plans together.'

'They'll be after you, too. Somehow it's going to get back and then they'll be looking for a Canadian. Your voice stands out. Also, they'll know your name.'

'You think Ellis Pearce is my real name? Do me a favour, ma'am. I thought we'd established I was no greenhorn.'

'Then what is your real name?'

He chuckled and pulled her to him. 'You'll find that out when you meet my folks.' Then, 'Well, that's our future fixed but meantimes we gotta get this particular wagon moving.'

He pulled away and walked towards the drinks cabinet. 'This is going to be the last time we meet until it's all over, so before we part we must have a toast. To both deals. To the success of the heist – and to our life together.'

She pulled him towards the stairs, 'I've got a better idea about how to toast to our success.'

Later he was at the back door about to leave. 'From now on be careful,' she said, arms locked around him. 'Frank's due back tomorrow. I've told you, he mustn't see any connection between us. He'd just go crazy.'

'How will I know him?'

She smiled. 'Looks a bit like you. Handsome feller. But more on the dark, handsome side. His folks were Italian. A good-looker, that's why I fell for him. Similar height to you too.'

He grunted and shook his head. 'Looking for an attractive-looking feller is not going to get me very far.'

'He's got a scar.' She ran a finger slicing her left eyebrow. 'Here. White line running through it.'

'OK, I've got some idea what he looks like. How do I meet him?'

'Keep a discreet eye on the house.' She guided him to the front and walked towards one of the windows. 'This window, the right when you are

looking from outside. I'll open the curtains so.'
She opened them to give a six-inch gap in the
middle. 'That means Frank's home and in the
house.' She closed them and walked past the
door to the other window, repeating the procedure with the curtains. 'When these are parted a
little, so, that'll mean he's come home and is in
town. That way there's no need for us to make
contact.'

'Does he favour a particular drinking parlour?'

'Usually the Three Deuces.'

They returned to the rear. 'Well, this is it,' he
said. 'We won't be seeing each other till after the
job. Remember two days afterwards we meet up
in Denver.'

'I don't know how I'm going to stand being
parted from you for so long,' she whispered, once
more locked in his embrace. 'I have to give you
something for luck. Something to remember me
by. Like the damsels of old used to give their
knights. You know, a silken scarf or some piece of
lace finery to tie to their lance before he entered
the lists.'

'Well, *I'm* not wearing any lace finery, my dear.'

'Of course not. But you've got to have something. A favour they call it.'

She disappeared and he could hear her
rummaging through cupboards and drawers.

'Here,' she said, returning with a cigarette case.

'Now every time you smoke, you'll think of me.'
'I don't need keepsakes to remind me of you.'
He gave her a final kiss and was gone.

FIVE

Ellis was getting restless. Near the end of town he'd taken residency in a chair on the boardwalk from whence he could see the frontage of the Scarpellis' house. He'd spent the whole afternoon there, killing time, throwing the occasional glance at the windows. There was a limit to how many times a guy could read through the same newspaper and to how many cigarettes he could smoke before he felt the ants in his pants.

Besides, he was getting hungry. When the ants bit once too often he stood up and headed for the nearest restaurant.

An hour later he sauntered back to find an old-timer sitting in his chair. He was about to ask the oldster to move when he looked towards the house and noted there was a gap between the curtains at the right-hand window. So Frank had finally made it.

Instead of shifting the old man, he leant against a stanchion and lit a cigarette. The signal at the window meant that Frank was back but still in the house. That figured. If Frank was half a man, there was no way he would make the saloon his first port of call. Deprived of the feel of feminine flesh for six months he would have some deficit to make up.

Ellis had no idea how fast Frank was in the sex department. Was he an all-nighter or a wham-bang-thank you, ma'am? He drew on his cigarette and pondered on it. Either way those curtains wouldn't shift for a while. Figuring to save his backside at least another half-hour of getting numb, he turned and headed for a saloon.

But, by the second drink, his mind had got stuck on the image of the ex-con's hungry hands pawing Mrs Scarpelli's body. And he imagined what else the man was doing at that very moment. Hell, he didn't know the guy – but he was beginning to hate him.

The declining sun was withdrawing its rays, throwing the lights of the town into relief, when he went back to his vantage point. The right-hand curtains were completely drawn and a gap showed in the left-hand window. So the guy had finished his fleshly pleasures and had now moved on to pleasuring his gullet.

The northerner headed to the Three Deuces.

He pushed in through the batwings and went up to the bar. He took his time over the mug of beer and scanned the room. There was a clutch of card players at this end and, near a piano at the far end, a small group chatting. Amongst the latter he spotted a man with a scar, small but enough to leave a white line running through his left eyebrow.

He needed a ruse to get near the far end without looking too obvious. One of the benefits of spending his early days in an ice-locked town at fifty degrees below – too cold to go out and play – was being schooled in indoor pastimes. Reading and re-reading the books on the family shelf explained why he was a little more educated than most; and the existence of the family piano meant he could bash out a recognizable tune.

He sauntered up the room, placed his drink on the ring-marked piano top and began running his fingers gently over the keys. His action resulted in the occupants throwing glances his way before they returned to their conversation.

But his playing was not to attract attention, more that he could overhear their words. It wasn't long before he heard what he wanted. Somebody addressed the one with the scar as Frank. The description fitted, the man was called Frank; now all he needed was an excuse to get into conversation.

He stopped playing and twisted round on the stool. 'Did I hear one of you guys call another Frank?'

Frank looked across. 'What of it?'

'Not Frank Scarpelli?'

'Who's asking?'

'Ellis Pearce.'

'Never heard of you.'

'This is a stroke of good fortune. I must buy you a drink. And one for your comrades too.' He walked to the bar and looked back. 'What are you gentlemen drinking?'

'Beer,' Frank said, 'but I still don't see why—'

'Who is he?' one of the men asked, as Ellis ordered the refills.

'Dunno,' Frank said, 'but he sure talks funny.'

'Let me introduce myself,' Ellis said, as he placed the glasses on the table. 'Ellis Pearce, late of Denver.' He nodded at a vacant chair by another table. 'May I?'

'Sure,' Frank said. 'Anybody buys a round of Mr Barleycorn, we'll take his company for five minutes, won't we, boys?'

Ellis swung the chair across and sat down. 'Fact is, one of my pals said, if ever you're in Lauderburg, look up Frank Scarpelli and give him my regards.'

'Who's this pal?'

'Hal Johnson.' Ellis looked conspiratorially

from side to side and lowered his avoice. 'Uses the sobriquet of The Randado Kid.'

'Sobriquet?' one of the others questioned.

'Alias,' Frank explained in a whisper. Then, louder, 'How come you know Hal?'

'Let's say we are in the same business,' Ellis said with a wink.

'How is he?' Frank asked.

'His leg's still giving him gyp but he's making a dollar. That is until he ended up in the pen for a short stretch.'

'He been inside again?'

'Yes, but he's out now. He's doing OK. Leastways, last time I saw him.'

'Hal doing time . . . the old owlhoot.' Frank shook his head and chuckled with some kind of remembrance. 'This is a coincidence. Next time you see him, tell him Frank's just done a stretch too. Fact is, just out, got back to town this very day.'

'No say!' Ellis exclaimed, feigning surprise. 'Jumping crickets, this deserves another drink by way of celebration.' He returned to the bar and dropped a bill on the counter.

'This guy's paying faster than we can drink,' one of the men said when Ellis brought yet more full glasses.

'Nothing's too good for a pardner of Hal's,' Ellis said, nudging Frank's elbow. During the session he only took one drink himself, and when he'd emptied his glass he rose. 'Well, I'm stove up,' he said, stretching. 'Had a busy day. Must get my back on some bedsprings for a spell. Listen, Frank, when you've finished here, come over and see me. We might have something to talk about. I'm in the Republic Hotel. Should be worth your while.'

'What's it about?'

Ellis winked. 'Just come over when you can. Something I know you will be interested in.' He slapped the man's back. 'Good to know you're out. See you at the Republic if you've a mind.'

Ellis sat at a table in his hotel room playing solitaire. There was a new addition to his ordinary wear: a brace of guns on each hip. Unlike other lawbreakers he didn't normally advertise his proficiency with weapons. A good proportion of his jobs were of the con variety and guns weren't needed. But from the off, this one was not going to be in that category.

Half an hour on there was a knock at his hotel door. Ellis rose from the chair, and buttoned up his long coat masking his armoury.

It was Frank.

'Glad you could make it,' said Ellis, gesturing to a chair. 'Make yourself comfortable.' Then, when his guest was ensconced, 'You interested in making some money? Big money.'

'Could be. What's the deal?'

'I've got a job lined up and I need some men to work with. I'm just passing through, you understand. A stranger round here and I don't know who's who. But it happens that while I've been here I've come across an opportunity. I was in a hole about fixing it. I can't handle it alone and was going to give the job a miss, because if I left town to rope some of my regular partners in it would be too late. Then I remembered Hal telling me about some guy out here in Lauderberg. According to Hal the fellow was reliable. But for the life of me I couldn't remember the name. I had to rack my brain before I could recall it. Then I got it, Frank Scarpelli. As a result I been hanging around town, hoping to come across you. But there was no sign and I figured maybe you'd pulled your picket. So I was fixing to leave tomorrow because time is getting too tight. Then, bingo – I see you tonight. And your being inside explains why I couldn't locate you.'

Frank took out the makings and began rolling. 'So what's the deal?'

'This is the pitch.' And he explained the circumstances. 'You in?' he asked, when he'd finished. 'If so I need you to rope in another three. Must be guys you can trust. I tell you, Frank, I'm going out on a limb with this one because I make it a rule not to work with unknowns. But the haul is gonna be a real big one, so I don't mind cutting corners on my principles. The way I see it, you being a sidekick of Hal's, that's as good as having Hal himself. I know I can trust you and your decisions on who you rope in.'

'I still don't know whether this is for me. I don't want to offend you, knowing Hal and all, but you're still a maverick steer in these matters.'

'Listen, I'll put my cards on the table. I've pulled more big jobs than you've had hot dinners. And I haven't been inside yet. That means I know what I'm doing. So, the decision is yours. You can take it or leave it. I'll respect that. But I can live with missing the haul. It's big, but I've found there's always something new round the corner. Maybe you think the same. Maybe you don't need a big score.'

'How big?'

Ellis took a cigarette from his case and lit up. 'Depends on the cuts. I figure the job needs five in total. If you sign on, that's three more hands besides you. Doing the figuring, their end would be four grand apiece. I figure your pulling the team together merits a double paycheck, so you'd be pulling eight big ones. I don't know what your circumstances are, but that kind of sum must set you up for quite a spell.'

Frank's mouth went dry. Quite a spell? Eight grand would clear all his debts, including buying back the mortgage on the house, with a heap of change left over that would last years. Years! And stop his missus nagging him about his inability to pull a dollar. He'd show her!

He licked his lips in contemplation. 'Leave it with me, pal. I'll be back as soon as I can.'

Ellis lay in the dark in his hotel room and waited to be contacted. Mid-evening a knock sounded at the door. It was Frank.

Minimal words passed between them and they left the hotel. Frank took him to a rundown neighbourhood on the edge of town where they turned off the drag and approached a small frame house.

'This your place?' Ellis asked, feigning ignorance of Frank's circumstances, as they walked up a weed-strewn, bare earth path.

'No. Belongs to a pal of mine.'

'How come we're not meeting at your place?'

'Reasons.'

Inside, the shabby room was poorly lit by a couple of lamps.

'Well, these are the guys,' Frank said. 'That's Trench.' He nodded to a fellow reclining in a hide-covered chair. The man had a straggly beard turning prematurely grey which put him closer to sixty in appearance than his forty odd years. He gave the newcomer a perfunctory nod.

'And that's Stack.' Stack was younger with battered features that told he was no stranger to a few fights. His eyes had a fixed stare that bore into the visitor. There was no greeting either in his eyes or his unmoving body.

Finally Frank pointed to the third man, younger than the rest and with a touch of darkness to the skin suggesting Mexican ancestry. 'And that's Angelo.'

'Gentlemen,' Frank said by way of concluding introductions, 'this is the guy I was telling you about. Name of Ellis Pearce. He's gonna tell you about something you might be interested in.'

Ellis looked at the glasses in the hands of the assembled company. 'You got a drink?' he suggested.

'Why, of course,' Frank said, nodding to the bottle on the table. 'Trench, you're forgetting your hospitality.'

The grey-haired man hauled himself reluctantly to his feet and took a grubby shot glass from a wall-cabinet. He filled it and passed it to Ellis. 'So what's this all about?'

'Hold your hosses,' Stack said, his eyes still impassive, glaring. 'Before we start any chat, how do we know this guy's a straight-shooter?'

Ellis threw the rye to the back of his throat.

'Frank here will already have told you this is a heist,' he said with slow deliberation. 'Why the hell would I be letting you in on it if I wasn't a straight-shooter?'

'Stack's right,' Angelo said. He was a bantam of a man with all the jerky aggression of a Mexican fighting cock. The flesh around his eyes creased as though he needed to squint to get a clearer image of the man they were inspecting. 'What do we know about this feller?'

'I'm the feller who's offering you a stake in a job,' Ellis said. 'A big job. What more do you need to know about me?'

'We wanna know your credentials,' Stack said. The piercing eyes looked the visitor up and down. 'Them fancy duds, that funny accent. Hell, could be the law aiming to set us up.'

'Looks and sounds different, I grant you,' Frank said, 'but I don't smell the law.'

Stack's manic eyes swung round in the direction of the speaker. 'Listen, Frank, you're a pal of mine and we done jobs together. But you're fresh out of the pen and anxious to score. In that frame of mind, you could be tempted to sign on to the first half-ass scheme that comes your way. That could put us all in a passel of trouble.'

'I'm no lawman,' Ellis interjected. 'Get that straight. And this is no half-ass scheme.' He turned to Frank. 'Say, what kind of penny-ante bozos are you roping me in with? I thought you said you knew guys who wanted real money and were reliable.'

'Pay Stack no never-mind,' Frank said. 'He's just the cautious type is all.'

'Don't treat me like no kid, Frank,' Stack persisted. 'I still want to know more about this guy.'

'Listen, pal,' Ellis countered, 'In this caper I'm taking as much risk on you as you are on me.' He sighed. 'OK, you know of the Rio Grande train knock-over six months back?'

'Yeah.'

'That was one of mine.'

'What proof do we have?'

Ellis reeled off the names involved.

'Hell, he could have read them in some newsheet.'

Ellis shrugged. 'Of course, I could. But that's all the credentials you're gonna get from me. Take it or leave it.'

'You ever been in the pen? Stack persisted.

'No, and I don't intend to break my record.'

'He knows the Randado Kid, too,' Frank threw in.

'How is Jake?' Trench asked.

Ellis smiled at the attempt to trip him up. 'His name's Hal and he was OK the last time we shared some barleycorn together.'

'I figure he's genuine,' Frank said. 'Otherwise we're gonna jaw all night and get no place.'

'And that sure is a funny accent you got there,' Angelo observed. 'You from the East?'

'Something like that.'

'Sounds more like Canada to me,' Trench said.

'We ain't here for a geography lesson,' Frank grunted impatiently.

Ellis shrugged. 'Frank, this conversation is getting boring. I'll give you fellers a minute to decide whether I'm legit.' He took out a cigarette, lit it and looked at the end while he waited. Then, 'Do we continue?'

The other four had exchanged glances which led Frank to the conclusion that the subject was behind them. 'OK, Ellis,' he said. 'Carry on.'

'Now we've got that out of the way,' Ellis said, 'we gotta get one thing straight before I go into details. There's going to be no cuts or percentages. You're going to be hired to do a job and you'll be paid for it handsomely. Whatever's left, high or low, is mine. My return for fixing the job.'

'And it'll be more than we get,' Stack concluded.

'I hope so,' Ellis said. 'But that's the risk I'll be taking.'

'Hell, why should you get the best end?' Stack demanded.

'I'm the ideas man,' Ellis answered, 'and I do

the financing, that's why.'

'What financing?' Angelo asked.

'For starters,' Ellis said, 'you're going to need clothes and horses.'

'I got my own bronc,' Stack put in.

'It's a local job,' Ellis explained. 'In a small place like this a man can be recognized as much by his horse as his clothes. So we're all gonna need different duds and mounts – for which I'll be paying.'

'OK, you take your expenses out of the haul,' Stack said. 'Then we divvy up. Listen, mister, we ain't dogs under the table waiting for scraps.'

'Half,' Ellis snapped. 'It's my operation, I'm doing the planning and the financing. There's plenty in it for your take, four grand apiece.'

Mention of the figure caused eyebrows to rise and appreciative looks to be exchanged.

'That'll put you in clover for the next ten years,' Ellis went on. 'You don't like it, say so now and I'll say thanks for the drink and get the hell out of here right now. There must be some other guys in town who are more amenable to the notion.'

He stood up as though going for the door. 'And you keep your lips buttoned about what little you've heard.' He patted his gun handle. 'You tell the law or anybody, you'll regret it.'

Frank laughed nervously. 'Listen, fellers, we're

all friends here. Let's keep it that way. OK. Ellis, it's your show. What you say goes. All right, fellers?'

Ellis waited until he had got agreement in assorted statements and nods, then returned to his seat to spell out the details.

'Let's get one other thing straight,' he said, when he'd finished and answered questions. 'This is a big-time job because I'm used to the big time. And I've done big-time jobs with some good buddies. The only reason I'm not roping them in on this score, is because it's cropped up quick and there isn't enough time. The point is there's a passel of guys out there who owe me favours. I'm the lone boy here and you four know each other. So I'm gonna lodge a note.'

He could see the spot he might end up in and had borrowed the idea of his ploy from Mrs Scarpelli. 'So, if you have second thoughts about my take once we've finished this caper, and it gets around something's happened to me, the note's gonna get passed on to the right quarters. These pals of mine are capable of doing whatever is necessary. And they're persistent types. The upshot would be you're gonna have to keep looking over your shoulder for the rest of your short life. And, believe me, it will be short. My pals are not only capable of violence – they enjoy doing it!'

He finished with a smile. It was cold and stern, but a smile. 'But I'm sure we're gonna keep this on a friendly basis, aren't we, boys?'

He looked at Frank. 'One chore needs fixing before the job: the telegraph lines out of town need to be cut.'

'I can handle that,' Frank said.

'OK, we ride out tomorrow,' Ellis concluded. He nodded to the bottle on the table. 'Shall we drink on it?'

SIX

The loaded stage rolled along the dusty trail, leaving its mark underneath billowing dust clouds. Up on the box, Florida Jones handled the lines while Brill Williams sat with his Sharps at an angle, the butt resting on the seat. It had been a good run and mid-morning the coach was hitting the plain at a fair lick on its approach to Big Fir Pass. Treeless, and dotted with patches of mesquite and organ pipe cacti, the arid plain, with the sun still on the rise, was becoming an uninviting place, more inhospitable for man and wild life alike as evidenced by the creatures that were now seeking the shade of cacti and crawling or slithering under stones.

'There's the pass,' Florida suddenly shouted, as they plunged over a rise. 'We top that, then there's only ten more miles to do.'

Brill shaded his eyes. Away on the horizon

across the plain he could just make out the crack in the rocks that marked the pass.

Inside the coach, the courier, a metal box chained to his wrist, was leaning his head against the side, his eyes closed. Opposite sat the extra guard the bank had laid on.

'What was that?' the courier asked, eyes opening at the sound of the voice.

'Guy said something about ten miles to go.'

'Thank God for that,' the courier said and rubbed his wrist. 'I'll be glad when this damn thing is offa me.'

As the coach lurched onwards he looked out of the window and noted that the passing monotony was now being broken by the rock formations that began to appear along the trail.

While they were still on the flat, Florida's arm arched and swept down as he urged the team to greater speed with his whip in preparation for the oncoming grade.

The passengers felt the coach tip and lurch when it eventually hit the incline.

As they approached the actual pass, a gaping crevice between two towering rock faces, the grade got steeper; the great whirling wheels churning up shifting mountains of grey dust, the six-mule team sweating and straining against the weight.

Despite the twenty-four pounding hoofs the

coach began to slow.

'Hap, hap!' Florida shouted.

The vehicle was labouring up the increasing steepness when, suddenly, a shot rang out, the sound bouncing from one surface to another. Brill swung up the Sharps instinctively, his eyes raking the tops of the cliffs but could see nothing but rock punctuated with stunted scrub.

'Halt.' The command echoed along the pass. Florida continued with his 'Hap hap' as he flicked the reins like a crazy man.

Still no attackers were visible. Rifle fire crackled and Brill tried to level his gun in readiness but found he had difficulty hanging on to the seat rail.

'Stop!' came the cry.

Florida continued with his urgings as the team hit the worst of the upward slant. With the violent swaying, Brill had difficulty registering the facts as guns exploded again. Now shots seemed to be coming from the rear as well, and he looked back.

Riders had appeared from around some rocks and were now in pursuit. The foremost gained and Brill could see grey whiskers as the man's bandanna flapped about in the slipstream. The man got closer, determinedly firing a handgun, and began to draw level with the box. Brill managed to swing the Sharps round and pulled the trigger. The man took the charge full in the chest and caromed back out of the saddle.

Brill tried to line up on the second but the coach was now within the pass and some attackers were firing from way above. All he knew was, something blasted through his hat and skimmed the side of his skull. He retained his senses momentarily before he fell from the bouncing stage. All went black as he hit the gravel and rolled down to the bottom.

Seconds later another shot fired from above took Florida in the shoulder and travelled down through his old heart. He slumped sideways, then dropped from the box. Now driverless, the stage careered along out of control and was only prevented from upturning by hitting the rock wall which brought the lathered mules to a snorting standstill.

For a few moments the shaken courier peered cautiously out of the window taking an occasional panicky shot, but he couldn't see anybody.

'Ain't no use,' a voice boomed. 'You're surrounded and outnumbered. 'Throw out your guns.'

The courier looked back at his colleague. The fellow was slumped on the floor with blood pouring from his head.

'Do as he says, Jim,' the guard croaked. 'Hell, it ain't our money.'

'You sure?' the courier asked.

'I'm sure I need a doc,' came a failing voice.

The courier threw out his own gun. He picked up the guard's weapons from the floor and disposed of them likewise.

'That all?' someone called.

'Yes.'

'Then step out, slow and careful.'

'It's gonna be difficult getting out of here by myself,' he shouted. 'This thing is chained to my wrist and it weighs a ton.'

He slumped back, breathing heavily, and waited.

Eventually a bandanna'd face appeared at the window. 'He's right, boss. The thing's shackled to his wrist.'

'Help him down.'

Two men entered and heaved on the case. 'Jesus,' one breathed. 'He was right about the weight.'

When the three men had eventually managed to get outside, the courier slumped to the ground beside the box.

'Where's the key?'

'I don't have one.'

'Don't give me that crap,' Ellis snarled, and yanked at one of the denim pockets in the man's jacket so that the stitching gave.

'It's true. The key's been sent on to the bank separately.'

'Shit,' Ellis muttered under his breath. 'The dame didn't say anything about this.' Then, out loud, 'OK, shoot the lock.'

Frank put the muzzle of his gun against the lock and pulled the trigger. There was a deafening explosion and a metal clang but the thing didn't give. He fired twice more to no avail. 'Hell, it don't happen like this in the books,' he muttered. 'This is supposed to be easy.'

'Stand aside,' Angelo said. 'Let me have a go.' But all that his two extra shells did was crumple up the thing further. 'Figure this is some newfangled steel, boss.'

Ellis looked into the distance impatiently. 'We can't hang around all day. Even in a god-forsaken wilderness like this, there could be somebody who's heard all the racket and comes nosing. We gotta get moving. Cut his hand off.'

Frank's brow puckered 'He ain't gonna like that, boss.'

Ellis placed a slug in the man's forehead. 'Now he don't have no say.' He stepped back and nodded towards the corpse. 'Now cut his hand off.'

'What with?'

'A knife.'

'You didn't say nothing about bringing a cutter.'

Ellis looked around the bandanna'd foursome.

'Don't any of you owlhoots carry a blade?'

Noting the shaking heads, he walked over to the boot of the stage and undid the leather fastenings. He rummaged through the contents, eventually extracting a shovel. He examined the edge, then brought it over. 'That should do it.'

None of them looked eager to take on the task. Then Angelo stepped forward. 'Shouldn't be no problem. I ain't worked in a slaughterhouse for nothing.'

'I can't watch this,' Frank said, and staggered away.

'Then make yourself useful,' Ellis grunted. 'Check the others. Tell me the body count.'

He jabbed a finger in the direction of the stage mule-team. 'Stack, you unharness them critters and scoot 'em.'

Frank looked inside the coach. Blood had pooled over the floor. He leant in and felt for the pulse of the guard. None.

He walked around the others, hearing the noise of Angelo hacking but trying to avoid the sight of it. Further down the grade he inspected Florida's crumpled body. He couldn't see much of a wound, but there was no doubt the oldster had driven his last team. On the way back up he looked over the side of the incline. At the bottom lay the shotgun rider, his Sharps some distance from his still fingers. He assessed the steepness of the descent to where the body lay. Easy to get down no doubt, but the loose scree would make it one hell of a mother to get back up. He'd have to walk some distance back to make the return.

But his decision-making was cut short by Ellis shouting, 'Come on, Frank. It's all over.'

Frank strolled back up into the pass, averting his gaze from the gore.

'Wrap the box in canvas or a tarp,' Ellis was instructing. 'Just in case we run into any nosy bastards. Then rope it to a horse.' He looked back at Frank. 'What about the others?'

'None of 'em are gonna give us any more trouble, boss.'

'Dead?'

'Dead.'

Ellis shrugged without expression. 'I didn't intend mass slaughter but if that's the way it's panned out, tough.'

Some minutes later, Stack and Angelo had got the box roped across the saddle of a horse. Stack wiped his brow. 'That is some weight, boss. And there's no way anybody can get up there and ride with it.'

'Then we'll run it in tow.'

'Look at it,' Stack replied, pushing at it to demonstrate its instability. 'Five minutes of jolting and it'll come away. There's no way to tie it securely. It's too heavy and awkward. Somebody's gonna have to walk with this baby.'

Ellis looked agitatedly across the plain again. 'However we do it, one way or another we gotta make ourselves scarce.'

'Hey, a chunk of the juicy bone in that thing is mine,' Angelo said. 'One of us walks with the horse, we all walk.'

'So be it,' Ellis said, exasperation toning his voice. 'But let's git.'

As they walked their horses out of the pass they neared the body of their fallen comrade.

'Poor old Trench.' Frank said, looking down at the crater in the corpse's chest. 'Poor bastard never knew what hit him.'

'Look on the bright side,' Stack said, mounting up. 'One less to divvy up with.'

Frank continued to look down at the body. 'Hold on there. What we gonna do with him?'

'Hell, leave him,' Ellis said. 'Come on. I've told you; we gotta get some miles behind us.'

'It's OK for you,' Frank continued. 'You're gonna be skeddadling back to Canada or wherever you come from. But once Mosely and the law get out here, Trench will be identified as coming from Lauderburg. That'll give the sheriff the idea it's a local gang. That's gonna put me and the other boys in a spot when we go back.'

'Hell, I ain't going back,' Angelo said. 'Once I've got my piece of the action I'm away. Nothing in Lauderburg to hold me.'

'Well I got a missus there,' Frank said. 'I gotta go back.'

'Hey, Frank's right,' Stack put in. 'Lord knows, I got no love for the place and wouldn't miss it if I have to steer clear. But my old ma's still there and I don't wanna get picked up the first time I go a-calling back there.'

'No problem,' Angelo said, pointing back at the pass. 'A couple of blows with one of those rocks over there would make his face unrecognizable.'

'You could do that?' Frank asked. 'To Trench, our buddy?'

'Hell, I liked him as much as you did,' Angelo retorted, 'but he ain't Trench no more. He's a hunk of meat with a hole in his carcass. Of course I could do it.'

'Don't see why Angelo couldn't do it,' Stack added. 'If he can chop a hand off with a shovel he can smash up a dead man's face.'

Frank shook his head. 'It wouldn't do any good. Trench could be recognized by his clothes, or something about his body that we haven't noticed. He's got tattoos for a start. I've seen him in the tub. No, we gotta take him and bury him someplace deep and out of the way.'

'That's going to slow us down,' Ellis said. 'We've got to get moving.'

70

Frank nodded to the box on the horse. 'That hunk of metal's gonna slow us down to walking pace. Having a tow horse with old Trench on ain't gonna be any extra handicap.'

'OK,' Ellis grunted. 'Do it your way. Get him across his horse and let's eat dirt for God's sake.'

'And we'll need the shovel for the burying,' Frank said. He returned to coach and picked up the shovel. With a wrinkled face, he scraped the end across the ground in an attempt to wipe away as much blood from the edge as he could, then joined the others.

SEVEN

The first thing Brill was aware of was a blinding headache, then the stickiness of blood trickling round his ear. He groped a hand along the smarting ache of his skull.

He picked up his hat, wiped away the tacky wetness from the inside and tried to set it back on his head. He winced and let it fall back on its retaining string.

He struggled to his feet, retrieved his Sharps and listened. No sound save the buzz of insects suggesting that the escapade was all over and that the bushwhackers had made good their escape. He looked up the grade. It was too steep to ascend, at least in his present state, so he walked back to where the incline was shallower.

His heart sank when he came across Florida's body. He knelt beside his old friend, verified the lack of life and sighed. Then headed back up the grade to the pass.

'Christ,' he breathed. Numbed at the sight that greeted him back at the stage, he hunkered down against the rock wall.

He took a breather while he considered what to do. Alone, there was little he could do here, that was for sure. He hauled Florida's body into the pass and laid it in the shade, then went to the boot of the stage.

For some reason it had been opened but nothing appeared to have been taken. He extracted the water bag, doused his neckerchief and freshened his face.

Then, with a last look at the bloody scene, he set off on the long trudge to town.

With luck, halfway back he met up with a homesteader's wagon heading to town. After he had recounted the incident, the two men exchanged few words. Brill still had a thumping head and the driver reserved all his concentration for getting his passenger to town as quickly as possible.

The banjo clock on the wall in the sheriff's office said ten minutes of one when Brill stumbled through the door. Sheriff Mosely was delving into a cold roast lunch. He was square-faced and durable-looking with the stiff bearing retained from his army days, a reminder of which was pinned to the wall behind him in the shape of a cavalry pennant.

He took the news slack-jawed. 'Jeez, it sounds horrific,' he said, when Brill had finished.

'You wouldn't believe it, Bob. It's looks like a battlefield out there.'

'Got any idea who it was?'

'No. It was all bandannas and guns exploding.'

'Know which direction they took off in?'

Brill shook his head. 'They'd made themselves scarce by the time I came to. When I looked around there was nobody – save for three men lying dead in pools of their own blood.'

The sheriff took his arm and guided him from the chair on which he had been sitting during his account and helped him to lie down on a horse-hair sofa at the other side of the room. 'You rest here, kid, while I get the doctor and do some organizing.'

Outside, he clapped his hands to catch the attention of some young boys playing with marbles in the dust. He instructed one to fetch the doctor, another to fetch the telegraph opera-tor. 'Ask Mr Goodman at the bank to come on over,' he told a third. 'Tell him it's important.'

A quarter of an hour later there was a bunch in the room.

'Sorry, Sheriff,' the telegraph operator was saying, 'line's down. Can't get any messages out.'

The sheriff nodded in receipt of the information. 'Reckon that's no coincidence. Let me know when it's fixed.'

The banker, Goodman, was sitting at one side of the desk, scribbling notes, there being little he could do apart from prepare a letter to his head office.

The doctor had cleaned Brill's wound, fortunately no more than a scoring of the surface skin. 'Nasty bruise on the side of forehead,' he commented. 'To my way of thinking it was the fall that put you out rather than the bullet. Might have a headache for a while, but you should be OK.'

Several more entered the small room, responding to the sheriff's call for a posse.

He turned to Brill. 'Think you can manage to ride out with me and the boys? I know it's a tough thing to ask, the state you're in, and I understand if you can't make it. But it'd be useful to have someone on the scene who was there.'

Brill got unsteadily to his feet. 'I can make it, Sheriff.'

'Got a horse?'

'No.'

'Easily solved. Collect one from the livery. Tell 'em it's sheriff's business.'

'OK. But I must go and tell Natty what's happened before she hears tittle-tattle and gets herself in a state.'

The sheriff's banjo-clock was striking two as he locked the door and accompanied Brill outside to join the motley cluster of riders awaiting him: a liveryman, a couple of storekeepers, a sawdust-faced carpenter and a saloon loafer.

'Beggars can't be choosers,' he muttered out of the corner of his mouth to the stageman as the pair stepped down from the boardwalk towards their horses.

'You weren't kidding about the place looking like battlefield,' the sheriff said, after he appraised the scene. 'We sure got some merciless *hombres* to contend with.'

He walked round the coach and noted that the flap over the boot was unfastened. He flipped it open and saw the untouched mailbag. 'Well they got some sense. Showing self-control like that means they were professionals. They knew enough to know that lifting the US mail would automatically get the US marshals on their tail. As it is, all they got to contend with is local law, unless they cross state or territorial lines.'

Brill grunted as he looked at the bag. 'Huh. The missus is worried about me riding shotgun and I've always told her as long as the line had the contract for the mail, we wouldn't be touched. So much for logic.'

'On the other hand,' the sheriff countered,

'you weren't to know one day you'd be carrying the sum total of a bank's assets in the back.' He pondered. 'Here, that makes me wonder how did *they* know?'

He eyed the rest of the contents. 'They take anything else?'

'Don't think so,' Brill said, rummaging through the rest of the odds and ends in the boot. 'Seems to be all here.' Then, 'No. That's funny. The shovel's missing.'

'Now we know why the flap was open,' the sheriff concluded, and walked back to where the other townsmen were laying out the bodies in an orderly fashion.

'They take anything from the deceased?' he asked.

'No, boss,' one of the men said. 'Not that we can see. The dead fellers have still got wallets and loose change in their pockets.'

'That means the critters were just after the big potatoes – the bank money. And keen to get the hell out of here.'

He turned back to Brill. 'You say you killed one them?'

'Yes. Just before they creased my skull.'

'Where did he fall?'

Brill thought on it, then walked back some paces, eventually pointing to the ground. 'Here. You can see the blood.'

The sheriff joined him and crouched down. He fingered the now dry, discoloured soil. 'You must have just wounded the critter.'

'No way. He was as dead as mutton.'

'How do you know he was dead if you went down immediately after?'

Brill wielded his Sharps. 'This is fifty calibre, Sheriff. It's designed to bring down buffalo. I hit the bastard square in the chest. One shot from this at close range, the guy wouldn't have any ribs or lungs to speak of.'

'OK, if he was dead why did they take him? Hauling the body along with 'em would only slow 'em down.'

'I don't know. Maybe so his kin could bury him?'

The sheriff gave a deprecating snort. 'Hell, no. These bozos are cold-hearted killers who knew the law would come after them. They're not civilized enough to have that kind of sensitivity.'

'Then why take the body?'

'Only one reason: because leaving him would present a risk. A risk greater than that of being slowed down by having a tow horse carrying the corpse. That means they didn't want him to be recognized. And that leads to two possibilities. Either he would tie them into a particular gang – or he was local, meaning the rest of them were local. My money's on the latter.'

He nodded back to the stage. 'That would also explain the missing shovel. They aim to bury him where we are unlikely to find him. At least for a spell.'

He turned from the spot and surveyed the rest of the scene, then shouted to get the attention of the rest of the party. 'OK, men. It's going take the five of you to clean up the mess here and render the stage roadworthy to get it back to town. That leaves me and Brill to take up the chase after the varmints.' He looked at the young shotgun rider. 'That's if you think you can tackle it, kid.'

'The varmints killed best pal. Try and stop me.'

'OK,' the lawman said. 'You say you got no idea in which direction they went?'

Brill shook his head. 'They'd clean gone when I came to.'

'Right, let's look for their trail.'

The lawman knew what he was doing. In his early years he had ridden scout for the army and had a keen eye for reading sign. He swung an arm indicating where Brill should start while he went off in the opposite direction. Then the pair of them worked methodically around the site in a large circle and it took less than ten minutes for the sheriff to find some hoof marks. 'Can't say how long these have been made,' he said, crumbling the earth between his fingers. 'But they're the only ones I can find so this is likely to be them. Come on, Shotgun. We got some riding to do.'

EIGHT

The miles slipped slowly behind the robbers as they maintained as fast a pace as they could with their encumbrances. Some time on, they topped a ridge and entered a valley. Ellis drew rein and contemplated the terrain. He noted a line of trees to the side.

'Don't figure they'd stumble on the late departed Trench if you bury him in that clump of trees,' he said pointing. He turned his horse in the indicated direction and the foot-dragging procession followed him.

While Ellis and Stack smoked, the others took turns in digging at a spot well into the trees. When the task was completed they heaped vegetation over the new mound of soil.

Ellis looked up at the sky. 'Day is closing in,' he said. 'Let's have another go at that box while there's still light.'

Stack and Angelo unroped the box, heaved the thing off the horse and thumped it down on the ground. When the canvas was removed Frank drew his gun and blasted again at the lock, once more to no avail.

Ellis knelt down and made his own inspection. 'I figure all you're doing is jamming the damn lock further. I reckon the weakest points are the hinges.' He took out his own gun, lined it up using his free hand as a shield, and pulled the trigger. Four shots later the hinges were smashed. 'I knew there'd be an easier way of doing it,' he said. He wrenched back the lid and exposed neat wads of bills.

The other three crowded closer. There were assorted noises of satisfaction while Stack's intense eyes were even more piercing. 'Let me touch it.'

Ellis stood up and went to his horse. 'You can touch it while you're loading it into the bag.' He extracted a bundle from his saddle-bag and unfolded it to reveal a large warbag.

'How much is there anyhows?' Angelo said. 'Seems somebody's gonna be getting a sight more than us out of this caper.'

'Remember the deal you agreed to?' Ellis snapped.

'I can't see why we don't just split it now,' Angelo persisted.

'I've told you before,' Ellis growled. 'We don't divvy up right away. That'll keep us together for a spell. Then none of you can go back to Lauderburg and start spending in a conspicuous fashion immediately after a heist.'

'So what do we do?'

'We ride further. Now we've dispensed with the box and Trench's body we can make some headway. We'll bivouac somewhere for the night, then keep riding and split the loot in a couple of days. That way those of us who aim to travel – like me – will have a chance to get clear of the territory safe in the knowledge that none of us has been caught and is spilling beans.'

He fixed the warbag to his own horse and reluctantly the others mounted up and followed him.

The land north was flat. Long grass dipped in the late afternoon breeze and the sun, lower now in the flecked sky, stretched out the shadows of the two riders.

The sheriff knew they were following in the wake of a trail, at least somebody's trail. But he knew his sign and was pretty sure the bunch ahead were the ones they were after. And there were around half-a-dozen horses. But neither of the pursuers knew what the men looked like.

Some miles on they spotted a lonely building.

The hens scratching in a fenced enclosure told them the place was inhabited.

The sheriff knocked at the door and was greeted by an elderly lady.

He touched his hat. 'Excuse us, ma'am. Did you happen to see any riders pass this was of late?'

She studied the badge that he had touched by way of explanation as he finished his question. 'No, son, I been doing the washing out back for most of the day. See, the weather's just fine for the drying.'

'Indeed it is so, ma'am. Is there anyone else at home who might have seen them?'

The woman looked back into the building. 'Fast Buck! You know of any riders passing today.'

'Can't say I do, Mildred,' came the response. The weak quaver in the male voice suggested someone of equal age.

'Sorry, son,' the lady said.

'Much obliged.'

'You look travel-weary, lad,' she added, as he turned to leave. 'It strikes me a glass of lemonade would be pleasing to you.'

The sheriff looked at Brill. 'Indeed it would, ma'am. Can't stay long but a quick refreshment would not come amiss.'

'You stay here. I'll bring it right out.'

The two hunkered down on the wooden stoop.

'What's going on, Mildred?' they heard.

'Don't you disturb yourself, Fast Buck. I'm just entertaining a couple of handsome young gentlemen with some of that fresh lemonade.'

'Fast Buck,' the sheriff said, when the lady brought out the glasses. 'Fascinating name that. Your husband, he been a runner in his time or something?'

'Oh, bless you, no,' she chuckled. 'Even in his prime, he was just about the slowest thing in the territory, man or beast. Saving maybe a tortoise. He might just have beat one of them critters in a race. But he's no hare. Like now, spends all his days in his rocking chair smoking his burley. Mind that's 'cos he lost the use of his legs years ago. No, they called him that because he was the local doc. That is before he retired.'

The sheriff finished his drink and rose to leave. 'Doc? I still don't understand, ma'am.'

'Since the days of Adam nobody's ever liked paying doctor's bills. Folks think they're just out to make a fast buck. Get it? A fast buck? Anyways, somebody called him that once and it kinda stuck. I cottoned to it and have called him that ever since. From my reading I think that's what they call irony.'

'I figure it is at that,' the sheriff said, wiping his brow and squaring his hat back in place. 'Much obliged for the drinks.'

'Any time, young man.'

The two mounted up and threw a wave as they moved away.

'Fast Buck,' the lawman muttered in a low voice, as they broke into a canter. 'What a name for a doddery old doctor in a wheelchair. Now let's see if we can cut some more sign of this bloodthirsty bunch before we lose all the light.'

It was getting dark when the bushwhackers spotted a clutch of ramshackle buildings nestling against a bluff.

Ellis reined in. 'What's that?'

'Oh, that's the old sling station for the stageline,' Stack explained. 'Dropped out of use when the line was transferred years ago.'

'Can't see any lights,' Ellis observed. 'Nobody uses it these days?'

'Shouldn't think so. Now the trail's overgrown, it's in the middle of nowhere on the road to nowhere.'

'Sounds ideal. Let's check it over.' They advanced some more then swung down from their horses to make their final approach on foot. Ellis indicated for them to fan out and moved towards the door. Taking out his gun, he eased the door back with his boot. The interior was dark and smelt musty, no smells indicating recent occupancy. When his eyes had adjusted to the gloom they confirmed his assessment. 'It's ours for the night, boys.'

Closer inspection with lighted matches revealed a rickety table and upended chairs There was a lamp pegged to the wall. Miraculously the dusty glass tower was intact but the fuel had long since been used up. Few windows had survived but it was not a cold night. They hitched their horses then made a survey of the environs. There was a sod house and a store with log walls like the main building. Crumbling fences marked where corrals had been.

Angelo came out of the store with a bottle. The vestiges of liquid sloshed around the bottom. He uncorked it and took a smell, then stepped triumphantly into the main cabin. 'I think we've got some fuel here, boys.'

A minute later the lamp was casting a glow around the interior, dim but better than nothing.

The warbag was in the middle of the table where all could see it. Chairs were straightened and they sat or stood around the thing, silently and in awe as though it was some deeply religious relic.

'Let's split it now,' Angelo said.

'The agreement is it stays in one piece.' Ellis said firmly. 'You remember the deal.'

'Well, at least let's count it,' Angelo persisted.

'No need to count it,' Ellis said authoritatively. 'You already know there's enough for your cut.'

'Well, I don't cotton to it staying in one lump,' Angelo continued. 'Like that it's easier for somebody to make off with it in one fell swoop.'

'Well, I'm not going to vamoose with it,' Ellis said, 'and have three fired-up guys on my tail, in addition to the law. And I hope none of you has the same idea either. I've told you, when I make a deal with a man I honour my agreement. I expect him to do the same.'

'You're right, boss,' Stack said. 'We're all in this together. We gotta trust each other.'

'Well, it stays on the table,' Angelo insisted, 'where we can all see it.'

'Now that's cleared up,' Ellis concluded, 'we need someone on watch during the night. There's always the chance that the law has organized itself quicker than I anticipated.'

There was a pause, nobody being keen on losing sight of the loot.

'OK, I'll take first watch,' Stack said, 'as nobody seems keen on volunteering.'

Angelo grimaced and rubbed his stomach. 'And I need to drop a load. Anybody see a craphouse around here?'

'No,' Stack said. 'But come with me.'

'Why with you?' Angelo said, following him to the door. 'It's som'at I can do on my own.'

' 'Cos you're gonna have to do it in the trees,' Stack said, 'and I'm gonna make sure you do it

88

downwind of the cabin. Remember, I've followed you in the privy before now. All that Mexican stuff you fill your guts with.'

The door closed behind them and the remaining two settled into a bite of hardtack and swigs from their water-bottles.

'I have to hand it to you, boss,' Frank said. 'You've planned this caper well.'

Ellis nodded. 'Maybe but I hadn't counted on a bloodbath. It's my experience that these stage-drivers – even their shotgun riders – don't reckon it's a good deal getting shot-up on account of somebody else's money. I thought that punching a few holes in the clouds would let them know we had guns and were prepared to use them, then ordering them to stop would have been enough. But can't be helped. It was their choice, their loss. Drawback is, that kind of body count will fire up the law some. Plus, any of us gets caught, it's crack-sure they'll do the kick-walk. Your boys have gotta realize that.'

'They do. You can post odds on it.'

'I'm not so sure. Particularly that Angelo. He seems a mite antsy.'

'Shouldn't worry. He's just a vinegaroon.'

'A what?'

Frank shook his head. 'I was forgetting. Coming from the snowlands you wouldn't know about such things. It's a scorpion we got down here. Puts out a juice smelling of vinegar, real sharp, hell, you wouldn't believe. Little feller, so big.' He indicated with his fingers. 'Looks, sounds and smells real mean, but he's harmless.'

'I hope you're right. But guys being antsy is why I'm not keen to split up the money yet. The longer we stay together, the less chance there is of one of us acting stupid and getting caught on his ownsome. You know your buddies: I don't. Might start blabbing the moment some piece of beef with a star starts bouncing his head round the walls of a cell.'

'I can see your point.'

Frank finished his snack and took a final swig from his water-bottle. He rubbed his lips then took out the makings. 'Hell,' he exclaimed. looking into his tobacco pouch, 'I'm plumb out of baccy. Hey, I've seen you smoke. You got a ciga-rette?'

'Of course.' Ellis pulled his cigarette case from his jacket, flicked it open and offered its contents. Too late he realized Frank's chatting had put him off guard. Probably deliberately.

Frank clutched Ellis's wrist with a hand knuck-led white with rage. With the other he wrenched away the case and snapped it shut. 'I thought this looked familiar,' he said, eyes glaring at the object. 'It belongs to my missus!'

He threw the thing aside, simultaneously

90

pulling his gun. 'That clinches it!'

'What the hell's going on, Frank?'

'There seemed som'at fishy about you from the start. The idea that the manager of the Lauderburg bank would tell a stranger about twenty or thirty grand coming in. Give me credit for some sense, pal. No matter how drunk he was, he wouldn't let slip information that important. And certainly not to a passing-through-town stranger. He'd have to be a complete idiot; and no matter what kind of simpleton a man might be, fact is you don't become manager of a bank by being a complete idiot. No, there had to be some other way you found out about what the stage would be carrying and when.'

Ellis eyed the gun. 'I don't know what you're talking about, Frank.'

'Yeah. Then there was your insistence on taking so much. I figure you're fixing to take off with half of the score. That was plain gall, Mr Pearce. Pushing the odds more than a mite too much. I been in the business long enough to know: when there's five guys involved in a job, nobody takes that big a cut. It's taking too big a chance 'cos when the chips are down it's gonna look like being too greedy to the other fellers. Some ways down the line one of the boys on a poor cut is gonna chaff. No, there had to be a reason – beyond being greedy – for you to take that risk.

The more I thought about it, the more the set-up smacked of there being somebody behind you. You were taking a cut for *two*. And that somebody would have to be somebody who knew the bank's workings.'

'I stipulated a bigger cut as the return for fixing the operation. It was part of the deal and you agreed to it. There's nobody behind me.'

Frank ignored the words and waved the gun muzzle in a ragged circle around Ellis's chest. 'Then, back at the heist you used the word 'dame'. You didn't think I heard you, but when you saw the chain on the box you muttered, 'The dame didn't say nothing about this'. At the time, in the heat of the moment, I didn't give it much thought – there was too much happening – but when the dust had settled I began thinking: what dame? Some woman working in the head office of the bank? Didn't figure so, because there would have been nothing to stop you telling us if that was the case. And, like you said, if you had got the details in Denver you would have brung some boys from up there. No, this was somebody you didn't want to talk about. That meant a dame in Lauderburg. And there could only be one. Seeing that cigarette case, now I know which dame.'

Ellis capitulated. Against such evidence he knew he couldn't deny anything. He thought fast.

'You're right, my friend. I didn't say it was your good lady who provided the information because I didn't want it to get around she was involved. She's taking a big risk staying in town. The finger of suspicion could fall on her at any time. Besides, she's a good-looking lady, Frank, and I didn't want you to get the wrong idea.' He nodded at the gun. 'The wrong idea like you're getting now.' He softened his voice. 'But there's no need for you to get riled, Frank. There's nothing between Mrs Scarpelli and me. It was strictly a business arrangement.'

'Like hell. I know my missus.' Frank's mouth quirked. 'You think you're the first to share her bed? Every time I been away, either in the can or away on a job, there's sign she's been bedding some stud. She might look the picture of decorum with all her finery and education but underneath she's all animal. One of those women who can't get enough.'

Ellis shook his head. 'You're surprising me, Frank. That's a side I don't know about.'

'I suppose you been romping in the hay while I been sweating it out in pen. Huh, she'd see you as a special catch. With your dude clothes, your fancy Canadian way of talking and your Canadian manners. Up there, you think you're better than us, don't you? Damn British Empire, God Save the Queen and all that crud. Well, there's only

93

two kinds of Canadians: thick-as-pig-shit dog-mushers and your kind – with your fancy clothes and smooth, "old country" manners.'

'You got things real wrong, Frank.'

'Yeah. You'd make a good couple in your finery. I suppose you were aiming to meet up and live off the hog-fat together.'

Ellis shook his head. 'I see I can't get you to see the truth of the matter, so what are you going to do?'

As the last words were emanating from his lips, he saw Frank grit his teeth, saw the gun move up. That was enough.

He dived to the side as a bullet zapped across the space where he'd been a split second before. And he rolled across the darkness of the floor as Frank's gun barked again. He pulled one of his own guns clear of the holster, jerked back the hammer and fired beneath the table. Frank crumpled to one knee as his bullet-shattered leg buckled. Ellis squeezed the trigger twice more in the direction of the shape.

He whammed the table out of the way to verify that three hits had been enough. 'And I *ain't* a Canadian, you wop,' he grunted, as he pulled his second gun. He stepped smartly into the darkness and levelled both weapons at the door.

Seconds later the other two burst in with drawn guns.

'Put your guns back in leather, boys,' Ellis said from behind them. They both knew they were disadvantaged. He had the drop on them, while he would be a poor target for them in the gloom.

'That's right,' he continued as they complied. They turned and he stepped into the light.

'Now you've holstered your weapons,' he said calmly, 'I'll do the same.' And he dropped his guns into place.

'What the hell happened?'

'Your friend here pulled his shooter on me, saying he was going reduce the cuts. I tried to persuade him, but he was trigger-happy. I managed to get out of the way and down him.' He knelt beside the body and feigned checking it. 'Poor, crazy feller. He's a goner.'

He stood up. 'I'm real sorry, boys. I know he was a pal of yours but I had no option. I figure sight of the money had turned his brain.'

The two men looked at each other. The account sounded genuine. This Ellis fellow could have gunned them down when they came in and he had now sheathed his weapons. Not the act of someone aiming to cut down on shares.

'Yeah,' Angelo said. 'Frank could be a real hot-head.'

'And what do we do now?' Stack asked.

'What's done is done,' Ellis said with a sigh. 'We bunk up here for the night, then share out in the morning. I'd feel safer if we still stayed together a piece longer. I'd like more time to get out of the territory, but in the circumstances, I can understand if you want to go your own separate ways tomorrow.'

'And what happens to Frank's share?' Angelo asked. 'And Trench's?'

Ellis sighed again. 'Their getting killed was no part of my plans. I'm a man of method. I'd budgeted a greater percentage for manpower expenses – that means paying you boys, all four of you – and I don't see why I should benefit from the demise of our partners, so you two share their cuts.'

The two men looked at each and exchanged nods, showing acceptance of their sudden good fortune.

'Now, we still need someone on watch during the night,' Ellis continued. 'We'll take it in turns.' He gestured to the body. 'After the business with poor Frank there, I've got no sleep in me now. I'll take first watch.'

'And the money stays in here,' Angelo said.

'Of course,' Ellis replied. He picked up Frank's rifle, checked the loads and headed for the door. 'Maybe one of you guys could relieve me around midnight.'

Angelo waited until the door had been closed behind Ellis. 'You think he can be trusted?'

'I figure he's genuine. If he wasn't, he would have blasted us when we came through the door. If he took Frank when he'd got the drop on him he can handle his guns and could have took us easy. And look how he's left us together with the money. Yeah, I think he's genuine. Honour amongst thieves and all that stuff.'

Angelo pondered on matters. 'Since we started on this caper our cut's been getting bigger and bigger. Why not go for it all?'

Stack shook his head. 'Get that thought out of your head right away. Like the man said: he's a man of method. Everything about him speaks to the fact that he's been on big heists before and knows a few big guys. Remember, how he's laid descriptions down about us someplace if something should happen to him? The way he's acting I don't think that threat is pie in the sky. He thinks things through. That's his insurance. I tell you, I for one don't want to take the chance. I want to get my cut and enjoy spending it someplace – without the notion that some unknown hardcase is gonna walk in and zap me.'

'Yeah, you're probably right,' Angelo said. 'As usual. But I'm still gonna keep my gun handy.' He stretched. 'Well, the quicker I get to sleep, the sooner I'll get my cut and be outa here.'

Stack looked down at the body. 'Before you lay

down your pretty head, give me a hand to get
Frank into the backroom. I ain't gonna be able to
sleep with his dead eyes looking at me.'

NINE

Previously, out on the open plain the two mantrackers had been making headway. They stopped, as was their practice, and the sheriff dropped down. He scouted a wide circle. 'Hell, we seem to have lost them.' The increasing darkness wasn't helping. 'It's a fool's errand to make any further progress without being sure. We'd best backtrack to the last time we cut sign.'

They did so, once again dismounting and scouring the ground in their usual methodical circle. Many minutes on the circle was almost completed when the lawman squatted on his haunches someway to the right. He strolled over to his companion and extended his hand. 'A cigarette butt. Ain't much of a guide but it still smells of tobacco so it ain't had much dew and drying out. That means it's only been dropped within the last day or so. You find anything?'

'No.'

The sheriff studied the butt before flicking it away. 'Well, that's the only thing we got. Might mean nothing at all. But if it is our boys it looks like they turned here and headed for those rocks. It's a long shot. You game?'

'I ain't come all this way to turn back now.'

They remounted and spurred their horses towards the gap. When they'd passed through, the rocks opened out onto a deep valley.

'I think we might be right,' the sheriff said, during one of his regular dismountings. 'Somebody's not far ahead of us.'

Brill joined him and looked down in the direction indicated by the sheriff's finger. There was a gob of phlegm on the ground. More important just above it a thin cobweb of spittle hung from a grass stem. 'Now that's as recent as you can get. Our long shot's paid off.'

They peered ahead but could see nothing, so hauled their backsides once more onto the leather and moved on.

'Hey, I recognize this,' Brill said, after they'd ridden another spell. 'This is the old stage trail. When I first started I used to ride shotgun along here. But not for long because they changed the route.'

'Can't see much of a trail.'

'No, you wouldn't. Fell into disuse years ago.

The trail was somewheres over on the right but it'll be all growed over now.'

Now and again the sheriff would continue his practice of dropping down and examining the ground. Sometimes there was nothing, sometimes a scuffed rock. Not much to go on. But the horse manure was another story.

'Something mighty odd here,' he said, turning over a lump with a stick, then breaking it. 'There's a lot of this stuff. Fairly new too.'

'What's odd about horse droppings? We've figured there's at least half a dozen horses.'

'Even for half a dozen there's a lot. See, it's the frequency. There's more than there should be. Whoever came this way are walking their horses. If the ground was softer I would have spotted it earlier. But I've suspected that for some time. Now I'm certain. So, keep your weather eye open and your hand on your gun butt because if it's our boys we're gaining on 'em!'

A quarter-hour on, he spotted some more manure. Dropping down, he took off his glove and placed his palm over it. 'This un's still warm,' he said in a lowered voice. 'I figure we're as close as we can be to 'em without riding plain up into their ass-holes.' He looked ahead. 'They could well be in sight now. See anything?'

From the higher vantage point of his saddle Brill strained his eyes through the gloom. 'No.'

'Well, if they're casting an eye back, as they should be if they know what's good for 'em, it's gonna be damn difficult for us to sneak up on 'em unobserved. We're too exposed.' He waved a hand to their left where the rocky side of the valley rose steeply. 'From this point on I reckon we should hug the side of the valley.'

When they got there, the lawman dismounted and kicked the gravel. 'Ain't good riding ground. We'll walk from this point on.'

A quarter-mile on he stopped. 'You hear that? Could be shots.'

'Yeah. But if they were gunshots they were muffled.'

They stayed still, angling their heads as they attempted to pick out any more sounds in the darkness; but heard no more. They pressed on cautiously, trailing their horses.

'Over there,' the sheriff suddenly whispered. 'Some buildings. Looks like a faint light at the window too.'

As they neared under the shadow of the bluff, they saw some tethered horses. 'Figure that's them all right,' he said. 'But can't see enough horses.'

'Maybe they've split up.'

'Or there are more horses in back. Come on, let's investigate. Before we think about announcing ourselves we gotta find out the lay of things and how many there are. I know you're all fired up, but don't start shooting impetuously at the first guy you see.'

He loped the reins over a branch and looked up at the night sky. The moon was clouded over. 'We'll leave the horses here and cross the valley. It's open but it's dark and there's a little cover in the scrub dotted about. And keep your eyes open for a look-out. If it's our boys they'll be wary enough to have posted one.'

Brill opened the breech of the Sharps and slipped in a four-inch shell.

It was midnight and Stack had just taken over the watch. Rather than station himself near the cabin with his back to it he had crossed the valley and was in the trees. That way he could monitor both directions along the floor of the valley while keeping an eye on the cabin. He was still uneasy about Frank getting shot. He figured the odds were on Ellis being genuine, but there was a heap of money at stake and that could turn anybody's mind, even Angelo's. On the off chance bullets started flying again he wanted see where they were coming from.

And it was because of his position that he saw the figure crossing the valley floor. He had no idea who it could be, but the furtive way the guy was moving from scrub to scrub, it didn't look like he had friendly intentions. Trouble was it was too dark to get a good bead.

There were clumps of vegetation close by. He would play the same game to get closer. At a crouch he moved out and made the cover of the first bush. As he neared he could make out that the fellow was carrying a rifle. Yeah, he was no passing pilgrim. Then, as the man loped to the next bush, the cloud shifted and the man could be plainly seen. Stack sighted, taking his time, and squeezed down on the trigger.

The sound racketed along the valley and his target pitched forward.

In the clear moonlight he could see the man wasn't diving for cover. And he'd dropped his rifle.

The door of the cabin opened and someone shouted, 'Stack, what's going on?'

'Some bozo was sneaking up on the cabin,' he shouted. 'Over there to your left. I got him.'

'Are you OK?' came the shout from the cabin doorway.

'Yeah,' Stack rejoined in equal volume and broke into a run towards the cabin.

But his diagnosis about being OK was premature. Brill had come in at the cabin from a different angle and Stack, unknowingly, was now running past him. Mere yards away a Sharps boomed and Stack was hurled several yards forward to land part way into the doorway. Ellis and Angelo fired into the blackness as they hastily hauled in their fallen comrade.

Just as they slammed the door shut there was a monumental crash and a chunk out of the middle of the door smashed back, crashing on the floor.

'Shit,' Ellis mouthed. 'Gotta be the law.'

There was another explosion and the whole window frame got blasted in.

Angelo shook splintered glass from himself. 'Whoever it is, they got a frigging cannon out there.'

'You see how many?'

'I don't care. I'm off. Thank God some of the horses are hitched out back.'

Ellis joined him and chanced a couple of shots through the hole where the window had been; not aimed, just to give their attackers something to think about.

The result was a series of pistol shots through the open space.

'Jesus,' Ellis mouthed.

'What we gonna do about Stack, boss?'

'For Christ's sake, look at him. He's got no more worries. That bloody thing's cut him in half. Sounds like there's a frigging army out there. You're right, all we can think of now is saving our own skins. And quick.' He heaved the warbag off the table. 'Throw some lead their way while I get this out back.'

When he returned, an exchange of fire was still taking place. 'We're OK so far. There's no one round the back yet. We could just make it.' He smashed the bottle of fuel onto the floor.

'What you doing?'

'Burning this place down. If we can get clear, we don't want Stack and Frank's bodies to be recognized, do we? Besides it might act as a diversion.'

He threw down a lighted match. 'Now let's git.'

Outside, Brill was circling the cabin when he heard the sudden pounding of hoofs on the opposite side. He moved quickly round and let off a couple of pistol shots into the darkness. But he could tell by the quickly receding sound it was to no avail.

By the time he had returned to the front, the interior of the building was already illuminated by growing flames. There would be nobody in there. At least not alive.

Still holding his gun he moved across the valley to where the sheriff was lying. He knelt down and could hear breathing. 'Where'd they get you?'

'Side of the chest. What's happened?'

'Got one but the others made off. Sounded like there were two. But more important, let's have a look at you.'

He tried to inspect the damage but the moon had clouded over again. 'Listen, it's too dark to see how bad it is and there's not much I can do here. If I got you into the saddle, you think you could ride?'

'Yeah, but not far. But I don't think I could make it back to town.'

'I wasn't thinking of town. Just as far back as Fast Buck's, remember?'

'Oh, yeah,' the sheriff wheezed. 'The doc.'

'Right. Now I'd say that's providence, having a doctor close by when you need him.'

An hour later they drew up at the little homestead.

Brill dismounted and went back to his friend.

'Are we there?' the sheriff wheezed.

'Yes.'

'Jesus be praised. I tell you, Brill, I don't think I could have made it any further.'

'Don't worry. Just stay there. I'll explain the circumstances. The doc should soon be able to do whatever's necessary. You're gonna be OK, Bob.'

The sheriff remained slumped in the saddle while all he could hear was the drone of distant voices. Something wasn't quite right because the conversation at the front door seemed to go on interminably and it was all he could do to prevent himself from collapsing on to the compacted soil of the yard.

Eventually Brill returned. 'We'll soon get you inside.'

He helped the lawman down and pulled the man's arm over his shoulder.

'What was all the jawing?' the sheriff croaked, as they lurched towards the light coming from the door.

'There's a couple of drawbacks, Bob. First off, the old guy was a horse doctor, not a genuine sawbones.'

'That ain't so bad. When you get down to it, hoss or human, it's all the same thing. Bone and muscle. He'll know what he's doing.'

'Yeah, but that ain't all. He's blind.'

Despite his condition the lawman managed to emit something like a faint chuckle. 'What was that you were saying . . . about it being providential . . . having a doctor close at hand?'

Brill grunted, adding, 'Yeah. And I also remember somebody saying something about irony.'

They stayed over the night. The medical provision was not as deficient as they thought at first bluff. The woman had been the veterinary surgeon's assistant throughout his career and had known what to look for when he asked pertinent questions. Also, in common with barbers out West, horse doctors had much experience of treating human beings as a matter of course; so, despite the fact that the couple were in their seventies, the sheriff was in capable hands.

The bullet had ripped away a little flesh and scored a muscle. Being the nearest person with any medical background, locals still called upon the doctor's services from time to time. So not only did the old fellow still keep his hand in, he prided himself on being aware of the new antiseptics and had some in his cupboard. After cleansing and medication being applied the sheriff had been bandaged and given the bed of one of the couple's offspring who had long since grown up and left.

Come morning, Brill visited the sickroom to see how his companion had fared.

'How you feeling?'

'OK. But I ain't gonna be able to move for a spell.'

'You don't have to. They said you can stay as long as necessary.'

'Looks like it's the end of our chase.'

'Like hell it is. I'm going after them.'

'Don't be crazy. They might only be down to two, but it's still a job for a professional.'

'I'm still going after them. Swear me in as your deputy.'

'Hold your hosses, Brill. I've seen you shoot at the annual fair. You're a good shot and no mistake. But there's a world of difference between shooting clay pipes and lining up on a man. Especially one with a gun in his hand who don't want to be took.'

'As far as I'm concerned these bozos are clay pipes ready for snapping.'

The sheriff frowned. 'Now, that ain't the attitude for a lawman. You've got to apply justice and work by rules. Suspects have rights to counsel and a trial. You've gotta remember, they're still suspects till they're proved to be otherwise.'

He exhaled noisily, wincing in the process. 'Besides, you can't go after hardened criminals on your own. This doing is too big. They ain't penny-ante thieves rolling drunks in the alley. It's a job for the territorial marshals.'

'Yeah, and how long is it going to take to get *their* asses moving. It would take time as it is, but now the telegraph's down it'd take days, a week yet. Listen, Bob, if you don't swear me in, I'll go without your blessing.'

The sheriff studied the man and sighed in exasperation. 'I can see your mind's set. OK, let's do this properly. The deputy badges are in my drawer back in Lauderburg. So you'll have to use mine. It's over there on my jacket.'

Brill unclipped it.

'I'm supposed to pin it on you,' the peace officer said, 'but I can't raise my arms. You'll have to do it.'

'Now hold up your hand,' he said, when the badge of office was in place.

The official necessary words were repeated.

'You understand what you've just sworn to?' the sheriff asked, when the oath had been administered. 'You've sworn to uphold the law of the county and territory. That means you don't take your own revenge. You catch a suspect, you bring him in.'

'Yeah,' Brill said half-heartedly.

Again a frown marred the sheriff's forehead. 'I ain't happy with the tone of that,' he said. 'Don't do anything stupid like using that Sharps on 'em without due cause. Otherwise, when my arm's better, I'll be obliged to haul you in front of a court. And I don't want to do that. I've known you too long.'

'OK. And thanks, Bob.'

The sheriff watched him fasten his jacket. 'Listen, I knows you're all fired up but you ain't got a monopoly on being affected by this. I knew Florida too – and his missus. With the old codger gone, most of the point of her existence has been drained away. So while you're at it, get 'em for me.'

Brill nodded. 'You won't regret this.'

'Hell, I hope not. God knows how I could face your Natty if anything happens to you.'

TEN

'Money's no good if there's nothing to buy,' Angelo said, head hung down in weariness.

They'd been on horseback all night. At the start they'd ridden as hard as they dared in the darkness, until they were sure there was no one on their trail. Then their pace had fallen to a walk; and now, fatigued horses and riders were moving very slowly through the early morning mist.

'I'd give a grand for a drink, a meal and a bed,' he went on. 'Especially a drink. Gee, is my gullet dry. I got the cash for it but there ain't nobody to supply the goods.' It was not the first time during their long journey that he had voiced some aspect of his discomfort.

'A grand?' Ellis queried. 'You'd fork out a grand?'

Angelo grunted without humour. 'OK, I was

exaggerating. But a hundred for sure.'

'Despite the truth of what you're saying, the horses' need for those items is greater than ours.'

'Who cares about these dumb critters?'

'I'm not a sentimentalist with regard to horses either, my friend, but they've been doing all the work. And if we don't attend to them pretty soon we can add the need for transport to our list of requirements.'

Shortly on, they came across a shallow creek. They allowed their horses to drink and graze while they refreshed themselves with the water.

'See,' Ellis said, as he wiped the moisture from his face with his bandanna, 'everything comes to he who waits. All that bellyaching and now you got what you wanted – free!'

Angelo shivered as the icy water flushed into the depths of his system. 'When I said a drink. I meant hot coffee. I just ain't myself in a morning until I got a couple of hot Javas swilling round my guts.'

'By that you mean your normal, pleasant self?'

'Yeah,' Angelo grunted, unaware of the cynicism in Ellis's tone.

They rested their horses for a short spell, then resumed their trek.

'Hello,' Ellis said, when they'd ridden but a few hundred yards. 'We got company.'

The mist had still not cleared and looming out of the chilly whiteness was the shape of a grazing cow. Then another.

In time they were passing increasingly more of the creatures. When the mist finally cleared they caught sight of a lone herdsman from time to time. On such occasions they would return the wave.

Suddenly Ellis reined in, stood in his stirrups, and squinted ahead. A tendril of smoke marked a distant camp-fire. He could make out several figures around a chuckwagon.

Angelo followed his gaze. 'The drovers' camp. Shall we skirt around it, boss?' He threw a glance back along their now clear backtrail. 'We don't know how close the law might be on our tail.'

'No. We're headed straight for the camp. Would look mighty odd if we suddenly made an obvious detour out here. And we don't want to arouse suspicions.' With that he urged his horse forward. 'Just act natural and leave the talking to me.'

Eventually they pulled up short and Ellis hollered, 'Howdy, the camp.'

'Hi there, pilgrim.' The speaker was an elderly fellow clad in brush-ripped range clothes, who had been watching their approach. He nodded to the simmering pan of beans. 'You're welcome to a bite to eat, friend.'

The two continued in and dismounted.

'That's obliging of you, sir,' Ellis said.

'But we'd sure relish a cup of that Java first,' Angelo put in.

'You're welcome to that too, friend,' the oldster said. He gestured to the cook who rummaged through his wagon for tin mugs and platters.

'You're the first folk we've seen for days,' the cowman continued, the tone in his voice showing his words were less of a statement, more of a question inviting some response. It was the code of the range that you didn't ask a man his business; but that didn't mean you didn't want to know.

Ellis stretched his aching limbs. 'We're riding north for work.'

'Yeah? What kind of work?'

'Anything that pulls a dollar.' Itinerant workers were the norm and shouldn't arouse any suspicion. 'Turn our hand to most things,' he added. 'Cattle work, for instance. You got need of a couple of drovers?'

'Sorry, pal.'

That was the answer Ellis expected and hoped for.

'Can't oblige,' the man went on. 'Got most of our miles behind us. We're on our last stretch to the railroad pens.'

Eventually the cook had supplied the visitors with cups of fire-hot black coffee and they hunkered down amongst the eating workers who eyed them with a lazy curiosity. One cast his eyes over their weary horses. 'You come far, stranger?'

Ellis's mind raced, trying to recall the local geography which was still relatively strange to him. 'Kentonville.' It was the first town he could think which didn't link them to Lauderburg. He rose and walked nearer to the fire, sticking his hands out seemingly to benefit from the heat but in fact to discourage more questions from the fellow.

They were served with overflowing platters of beans which they devoured with obvious relish. Finally Ellis slopped out the dregs of his second coffee and handed the mug back to the cook. 'Obliged for the hospitality, sir. Figure we must hit the trail again.'

'So longs' were exchanged and the two headed out, throwing back a friendly wave.

The elderly man watched them as they became dots in the distance. 'If they's working men I'm a monkey's uncle. You guys see their hands? Softer'n a baby's tush.'

'Yeah,' another drover said. 'And they wus lying about the trail they's on too. If they're riding north from Kentonville, they've sure lost their way to cut our trail the way they did.'

'Som'at else,' the older man mused. 'Ain't often you see fellers choosing to ride out into a wild no-man's land like this without provisions.

Hell, they weren't even carrying water-bottles.'
Then he shrugged. 'Who knows? Takes all kinds.
Come on, boys, back to work.'

'When we gonna split the take?' Angelo asked
when they were finally clear of the cattle drive.
'Nobody can see us now. It's about time I saw my
money. I'm getting itchy.'

Ellis squinted into the distance and could just
make out mountains breaking the skyline. Denver
meant rocky country. 'You're right.'

'Well?'

'Where you headed?'

'I been thinking about that. I got kin out in
Nebraska. North Platte. I think I'll pay 'em a visit.'

'Think you can keep quiet about your money?
It's not a few cents.'

'Sure. I'll buy a few presents but that's all.'

All his time alone with Angelo, Ellis had made
sure they were riding stirrup to strirrup. Rarely
had he allowed the man to get behind him or be
out of view. The guy might have been genuine,
but he didn't want to chance it. And when it came
to the final parting he wanted it to be on the flat
in the open where he could still see him. Ideally
a spot where the directions from their parting
formed a V so he could monitor the receding
figure from the side.

'You could strike out for North Platte from

here.' He looked at the sun, gauged the direction, then stuck out an arm. 'Thataways. North-east.'

'Yeah,' Angelo said. 'From what I remember the last time I saw a map, that would do it.'

'OK, pardner,' Ellis said. reining in. 'Get your saddle-bag ready.'

He dismounted and untied the warbag. He was in a dilemma. Just in case he had any funny ideas, he needed both hands free; hence he didn't want to do the divvying himself. If the kid counted out his own share, sight of the bulk might give him ideas if he didn't already have them. He compromised. He would give the kid a greater cut than he expected.

So, he placed it on the ground and stepped back. 'Go on, open it,' he said.

Angelo excitedly wrenched the thing open and stared at the contents.

'Before you go any further,' Ellis said, 'the deal was I take whatever's left after payments.'

'Yeah.'

'And if there was as much as I'd hoped in the box, that would be a large sum. Now, the reason for the bigger cut is because there's another person involved. Somebody I planned this with.'

'Who?'

'Doesn't matter who. The point is then I didn't reckon on most of the boys not making it to the payoff. So the fact is there's not two of us left, but three.'

'How much does that make for me, boss? I ain't too clever with my figuring.'

'Ten grand. That's a lot more than you were fixing on, wasn't it?'

'Yeah, sir,' Angelo said, wide-eyed.

'So we're agreed?'

'Yeah.'

'Then take the bundles out one at a time and slowly flick through each so I can see the separate bills. I'll do the counting if it isn't your strong-point.'

It took ten minutes. 'Those bank cashiers were spot on,' Ellis said, then instructed Angelo on cutting out his ten grand.

'Now I tell you your problem,' Ellis said, as Angelo stuffed the money into his saddle-bag. 'Those are all big bills and are hot money. They're going to be difficult to spend without arousing suspicion. Your best bet is to find some-body in commerce who'll take them, or some of them, at a discount.'

Angelo thought. 'Yeah. I know a fellow does figuring for companies and such. Straight as a dog's hind leg. Met him in stir.'

'I've not known you long,' Ellis said, when both sets of bags were fixed back in place, 'but you've been a credit to the operation. The cash you got there tells you that. Pity all your buddies got dropped along the way.'

'To tell the truth, we weren't that close.' Angelo chuckled at the thought. 'Just no-goods who bummed together at times to knock over stores and such. Penny-ante stuff.'

'Well so long,' Ellis said, and stuck out his hand. 'And, as they say, keep your powder dry.'

Minutes later they were making the intended V, Ellis keeping an eye on the figure gradually receding to his right.

About this time Brill ran into the cattle drive. Had they seen a bunch of men, no more than four but maybe as few as two?

'We not only seen two fellers,' the oldster explained, 'but they was mighty suspicious inasmuch as they told tall tales. Wasn't up to us to question what they said – they was just a-passing by, partaking of some of our food and coffee – but they was yarn-spinners plain enough.'

He recounted his observations, finishing with, 'Why? What they done?'

'Well, if these are the pair,' Brill said, 'they are the remains of a gang that bushwhacked the Lauderburg stage. Left a passel of dead behind while they were at it. So, is there anything you can tell me about them by way of descriptions?'

'One was slightly Mexican-looking,' the leader

said. 'Young, quiet feller.'

Eager to claim later around the camp-fire that they had made some contribution, other cattlemen were eager to chip in. 'Yeah, he'd got a bit of a squint to his eyes,' one added.

'The older one had some kind of accent but I can't pin it down,' another said.

'I can pin it down,' yet another said. 'I done some seasons cattle punching up near Calgary. They speak that kind of soft twang up there.'

Brill nodded. 'Canadian?'

'Yeah.'

When he had gleaned as much as he could about appearance, Brill asked which way they had headed. He was given directions to the site of the camp-fire, and then from whence the men had ridden.

ELEVEN

The leader of the Lauderburg stage bushwhackers had hit rough country with broken rocks and crags. Some time back he had entered a canyon and was now threading his way between lofty bluffs.

More used to travelling by stage along prescribed routes he was relatively unfamiliar with the minutiae of geography and crossing country on horseback. He knew he was heading roughly in the direction of Denver but when he cleared the present rough stretch he was hoping to come across some kind of habitation where he could ask the way.

He was thinking on these matters when a rifle shot exploded. His horse reared and he pitched backwards to the ground. Another shot. From behind, high up on the cliffs. Chunks gouted out of the rock close to Ellis's head and he instinctively crouched against the granite wall.

More shots in quick succession. Triggered by someone intent on putting his lights out. It could only be one person – Angelo. The ungrateful bastard. Ten grand should have been enough for anybody.

Ellis's mind raced. It had been a long time since their parting so the jasper must have been working his way along the top, keeping Ellis in view, biding his time, waiting for the best opportunity.

Ellis cursed at having allowed himself an unguarded moment.

More explosions, and his horse eventually went down in a cacophony of whinnying, its foreleg shattered. Those shots had been deliberate. Angelo must have suddenly realized the gunfire could startle the animal into vanishing over the horizon – along with the money – and had put it out of action.

Ellis was still in the open and he looked around for cover. To his rear was the nearest possibility. He scuttled along to the accompaniment of more gunfire and dived behind the rocks.

He was pinned down and his horse useless. How could he handle this?

The warbag tied to the horse's back was Angelo's objective. How could the jasper be tempted down to come and get it?

If Ellis could feign being shot . . .

But it needed taking a risk. The thought that crossed his mind was that it had taken Angelo several shots to hit a target as big as a horse. Why? Then he remembered the bozo's squint. Maybe he had deficient eyesight, a deficiency he would-n't be anxious to boast about in his line of work.

Nothing else for it but to bet on this reasoning. He slowly raised his head as though recon-noitring, deliberately making himself a clear target. Then he ducked back before exploding rock ripped into his face. And, as he disappeared, he let out an almighty scream that would be heard the length of the canyon.

He took out both guns. Then he worked his way a little distance further back till he was tucked below a low overhang, so low there was barely enough room for his body. But it served its purpose of obscuring his body should Angelo peer over the low rocky rampart.

Just as crucial, he still had a good view of the horse. With both arms outstretched along the ground he worked back the hammer of each gun in preparation. Now all he needed was patience. Hopefully more patience than Angelo could muster.

All that could be heard was the caw of birds, the whirring of insects – and the angst-ridden whimpers of his horse.

He had no measure of time. But it must have been passing at some rate as shadows were lengthening along the rock within his limited sight.

It was noticeably darker still when he heard the faint crunch of a foot on gravel close by. Angelo must have looked over the rampart. And the man must have been satisfied there was no one there because the next noises were less judicious.

The moment the man appeared Ellis sent a succession of bullets into his frame. He wormed his way out of the fissure and lunged forward.

'Huh, some vinegaroon,' he scoffed, standing over the man. Giving the two-timing Angelo no more investigation than to confirm he was dead he placed his gun at the back of the head of his snuffling horse and pulled the trigger.

It took him an hour to retrieve Angelo's horse and to load it up with all the money and whatever other bits he could salvage.

The horse carcass was the first thing Brill saw. Up close he found the body of a man. He pulled away the hat and studied the face. He didn't know the fellow but there was some familiarity to the features. Moreover, it was a little too familiar for him to have casually seen the fellow during a stage run. Dismissing that notion, the only conclusion was the guy was from Lauderburg.

That fitted in with Bob's theory. It had been a local gang.

One other thing he learned from the scene.

There was only one of the bushwhackers left. And he was a Canadian. But that was all he was going to learn.

The canyon opened out on to a vast plain. The Canadian could have taken any direction. He rode clear of the passage and, following the procedure he had learned from the sheriff, he slowly worked round a large semi-circle. But, unlike Sheriff Mosely, he was no tracker.

He took a long look at the rolling landscape. There was a handful of possible trails. It would be stupid to pick one in the hope it was the right one.

Disheartened, he turned around and rode back.

On his return journey he was finally guided through the darkness by the drovers' camp-fire and there he shared their bivouac for the night.

Next morning he called in at the home of Fast Buck to enquire about the sheriff's health.

'He's recovering well,' the doctor told him, 'but it's advisable he doesn't try riding a horse for at least another few days.'

Brill went on to acquaint the sheriff with his findings and his final coming to a dead end.

'You've done all you can,' Bob said, 'and I'm grateful for that. But you might as well hand in your deputy badge. Just one other thing you can do for me while you're wearing it: if the telegraph lines have been repaired when you get back to Lauderburg, pass on what you know to county and territorial law offices. It's their pigeon now.'

'I'll do that of course,' Brill said. 'But I'm not handing in my badge yet awhiles.'

'What else can you do?'

'When I get back to town, I can try to identify who took part in the robbery. Maybe I can get a clue to where the last remaining gang member is headed.'

The sheriff nodded. 'You might be able to identify them, but I can't see it telling you anything about where this Canadian's gone. He's an out-of-towner and we know nothing about him. He could be anywhere.'

'I'm still gonna try.'

'OK, if you're that determined you may as well use the office as your base. The key's in my jacket pocket over there on the chair.'

Brill frowned. 'If I'm going to be sitting in your chair, does that mean my duties will extend to catching and locking up drunks?'

The sheriff managed a smile. 'You're what is known as a *special* deputy. That means you're following my instruction with regard to a specific

case. No need to bother yourself with town misde-
meanours. Don't worry: that pain-in-the-ass
responsibility is mine when I get back.'

TWELVE

When he got to Lauderburg he went straight to the telegraph office. Now that the villain was likely to be beyond the jurisdiction of the local law it was even more important to inform the territorial peace office. But the lines still hadn't yet been reconnected. Next, he called in at the law office and, when he had spent a few minutes familiarizing himself with the place, he claimed some handcuffs from a drawer, lopped them over his belt and pocketed a piece of paper and pencil. At the bank he acquainted Goodman with his becoming the deputy and what had happened.

Finally he went home.

'I'm so glad you're taking off that terrible badge,' Natty said, as she checked his head injury. 'I was so worried when I saw you coming through the door with it.'

'Oh, it's not coming off yet, honey. The case isn't closed.'

'But you said there was only one of the desperadoes left, and he's on his way out of the county.'

'Until details can be gotten through to the authorities, there's only me in a position to do anything.'

'You have no obligation. Besides, what can you do?'

'Keep my eyes open. Ask questions.'

'Ask questions? You're not a detective.'

'I wasn't a lawman either till I put this badge on, but I'm learning.'

After a meal he began a tour of the saloons in an attempt to find out about any unexpected absences from town. The town was not large but, on account of the mining, it was characterized by a very mobile population with folks always coming and going. Around nine there was no room for any more names on either side of his sheet of paper and he gave up that aspect of his inquiry as a bad job.

Exhausted, he slept longer than usual into the next morning. Consequently the day was bright and sunny when he finally ventured out on to the boardwalk. He was going to try a new tack and see if he could turn up anybody who had unexpectedly come into some big money. There was a bracing wind sweeping in from the flats as he waved to his temporary replacement driver on the outward-bound stage. He waited until it had passed, then crossed the road.

From then on, he began his tour of the saloons. In each one he questioned about signs of anybody throwing big dollars around. But a couple of hours on, he had drawn no leads.

He came out of the last saloon, lit a smoke and leant on the rail to watch folks go about their business. Reconciling himself to the fact that he had spent yet more useless time, he crossed the street and headed back home for lunch. In doing so, he mounted the sidewalk and walked past the bank. A small notice fixed to the door flickered in the breeze. It held no importance but, some paces on, he stopped. Wait, it was a new notice and something didn't gel. He returned to check it and read: TELLER WANTED (TEMPORARY).

Yes, something was a little odd. If the bank's business was in decline because of its dependence on the collapsed mining company, why would they want another teller? Mildly intrigued and with nothing else to do apart from have lunch, he went inside.

Goodman was behind the counter poring over some document.

'Morning, Brill,' the man said, looking up.

'Any more developments?'

'No, sir.'

'Anything I can do for you?'

'That notice outside, what's that all about?'

'What it says. I need a teller.'

'I don't understand. If things aren't as busy as usual, why do you need *extra* help?'

'Oh, it's only while Mrs Scarpelli is away.'

'Mrs Scarpelli?' Brill vaguely knew her. 'How come she's going to be away?'

'Her sister over in Mortimer is sick. She hasn't been well for some time. It's not the first time Mrs Scarpelli's been out to visit with her.'

'How many times before?'

'Let me see . . . twice.'

Brill pondered. 'Did you get another teller on those occasions too?'

'No.'

'Then why this time? What's so special?'

'Because this time she'll be away longer. Her sister's taken a turn for the worse. Real bad, they say. So, she said she couldn't say when she'd be back and I was not to be concerned if it was a long time. I tell you, even though business is slack I miss Mrs Scarpelli's help. She's a real gem. Fact is, she pulls more than her weight. Don't know how I'll do without her.' He pointed to the document on the counter. 'Handles all the paperwork, like this. And she's a real whiz with figures. I sure hope she won't be away for long.'

Brill digested the information. 'Handles all the paperwork? Does that mean your correspondence? With your head office, for example?'

'All of it.'

'So she'd know about the cash shipment and all the details?'

'Of course.'

'When did she leave?'

'She tidied up and finished at the bank at closing time yesterday. Said she was fixing to catch this morning's stage.'

Brill snapped his finger and thumb in exasperation. 'Then she's been long gone. I saw the stage pull out earlier.'

'Yes.' The banker frowned slightly. 'What's your concern?'

'Just looking for something different. Like somebody acting out of the ordinary.'

'She isn't acting out of the ordinary. I've told you, she's been away before.'

'Has she ever told you before that she doesn't know when she's coming back?'

'No.'

'Then she's acting out of the ordinary.'

The banker's frown became stressed. 'You're not suggesting Mrs Scarpelli had anything to do with what happened?'

'No. I'm just trying to eliminate things. And that's why – next time you see her or are in contact with her – you don't mention my questioning.' Replacing his hat, he walked to the door. 'We don't want to disturb her unnecessarily.'

Out on the boardwalk he thought about it. Her travelling away could be all above board. Her leaving wasn't exactly out of the blue, what with her sister having a history of illness; and it being on record that Mrs Scarpelli had gone out to visit her on previous occasions. On the other hand, he was hitting a brick wall with his other lines of investigation. He had time for a wild-goose chase.

He dropped in to see his working colleagues at the depot.

'Hi, Brill.' the clerk greeted him. 'What's this I hear about you being on temporary secondment to the law office?'

'Yeah. And as the pay is better than I get from this place it might become permanent.' He motioned to the map on the wall. 'More important, George, have you got a map I can borrow?'

'Boss wouldn't cotton to me giving you that one off the wall but I've another someplace. What are you interested in particularly?'

'Mortimer and the area around it.'

The clerk finally found one and spread it out in the counter. 'There you are, Brill. And there's your regular Mortimer-Lauderburg stage route.'

Brill studied the map for a while, trying to work out where he'd travelled over the last two days.

Then, he concentrated on Mortimer. 'Out of Mortimer, there's a trail east or west,' he mused. 'And, north, the coach road to Denver.'

With a 'Thanks, George' he rolled it up and left.

Back home, he asked his wife to prepare some provisions for another trek north.

'I don't know what makes me more apprehensive,' she said, a shade of distress in her voice, 'you riding on the top of a stagecoach with that shotgun in your hands, or chasing after murdering villains with that tin badge on your chest.'

The early sun was still stretching long shadows when he set out the next morning along the northern trail. His mind was kicking around the puzzle of Mrs Scarpelli when he found himself riding up the grade of the southern entry to Big Fir Pass.

Once again the vivid images of the recent gory scene forced themselves into his consciousness as he rode through the gap. But clear of the pass, he was able to shake off the disquieting thoughts and concentrate on the matter in hand.

He still had some miles to go before he reached the town when he saw the first southbound coach of the day approaching. He waved the vehicle down, recognizing the crew as it neared.

'Howdy, Brill,' the driver shouted, above the clatter of the decelerating coach and its mules. 'And what's you particular brand of trouble this morning?'

'Yesterday, you had a woman passenger out of Lauderburg?'

'Yeah. That gentlewoman from the bank. Refined lady. What's her name?'

'Mrs Scarpelli.'

'That's the lady.'

'You notice where she went when she disembarked?'

The driver shook his head. 'No, I had some affairs to attend to at the end of the run.'

'I saw her, Brill,' the coach's shotgun chipped in. 'She picked up the link to Denver.'

With a 'Thanks, fellers' Brill gigged his horse onward.

Now he was surefire intrigued. Mortimer hadn't been the woman's final destination as she had professed. She was headed for Denver – or maybe further?

She was supposed to be visiting a sick sister in Mortimer. So why would a prim and proper bank employee lie about a straightforward domestic matter?

THIRTEEN

It was late afternoon when Ellis rode into Denver. Whether or not one believed the claims of its voluble mayor that it was the second biggest town out West after San Francisco, it was certainly big enough for a man to fade into the background.

He booked into a hotel as Tom Edson. It was one of the best places in town, its appointments the kind one might expect in a sophisticated metropolis, his large room being sectioned off with a cubicle containing a commode and tin bath.

Leaving the bulk of his kit in the room but toting his precious warbag over his shoulder, he walked through the town inspecting the stores. Eventually he found one where he could purchase a carpetbag.

Back in the hotel he folded the warbag as compactly as he could around its contents and eased it into the carpetbag.

He lay down on the bed, resting and thinking.

When the law got organized they would initially be on the look-out for two men on horseback. It was unlikely they would be looking for a man and wife travelling by coach.

The route was clear and familiar to him. They would travel north by stage and catch the west-bound Union Pacific at Cheyenne. There was at least a month before ice created problems access-ing Nome, so there would still be a wide variety of craft offering passage north out of San Francisco.

When he had rested, he went downstairs. In the lobby a young woman was registering at the desk. As he passed he couldn't help noticing the pretti-ness of her face surrounded by wispy curls. But as she looked his way, the eyes showed a certain weariness.

He touched his hat as he passed. 'Ma'am.'

She smiled and nodded in return, the tiredness briefly disappearing from the eyes.

Outside he looked up and down the busy street, till he spotted the depot some blocks down on the other side. He crossed the road, weaving his way between the bustling traffic. As he made his way along the boardwalk, in the distance unseen fireworks crackled. Somewhere, some-body was having a celebration. Denver was sure a bustling, noisy place compared to the tinhorn towns he had been used to for the last few months.

The depot office consisted of a small room with a counter, a couple of chairs and a large map on the wall. 'When's the next stage due in from Mortimer?' he asked the clerk. 'I'm expecting my wife to be arriving on it.'

'If it makes good time the old crate should make it by noon.'

'Well, hoping that she makes that particular coach, can I book provisional passage for two to Cheyenne? I'll confirm when the Mortimer coach arrives.'

'Of course, sir. But you realize that booking ahead, there'll be a deposit which is not refundable should you cancel.'

'Understood.' As he replied he thought of the fortune inches away from his hand in the carpetbag and added, 'No problem,' in a subtle tone that would have no meaning for anyone other than himself.

When he concluded the business, using the same name that he had put down in the hotel register when signing in, he crossed the room to look at a map on the wall. He took a cigarette from his case and smoked while he examined the chart, tracing his finger over the routes and connections.

While he was engrossed in the task, the young

woman from the hotel lobby came in and he heard her booking the same coach. When she moved to leave, he opened the door for her. 'Allow me, ma'am.'

Once his hand was free of the door he used it to touch his hat. 'Excuse me, ma'am. We're booked into the same hotel. I saw you earlier. If you're returning to your accommodation, I'd deem it a privilege if you'd allowed me to escort you there.'

'I'm a grown lady, sir, and can manage a couple of blocks by myself.'

'Of course. I'm sorry.'

Then she smiled, realizing the abruptness of her reply. 'Forgive me. I've had a tiring day and was forgetting my manners. Of course, you may escort me.'

'Thomas Edson at your service, ma'am.'

'Mrs Portia Robbins.'

Then, 'Have you made the northward trip before?' he asked as they walked.

'No.'

'Well, ma'am, you've got an exciting trip ahead. Mountain passes and all.'

Just before they got to the hotel he noticed a poster advertising an Independence Day Ball.

'What's the date?' he asked.

'Why the fourth of July, of course.'

'Well, I'll be,' he said. 'That explains the fireworks a while back.'

'Yes, I heard them too.'

'The truth is, ma'am, I've been so preoccupied of late I clear lost track of the calendar.'

Just before they entered the hotel he gently stayed her arm. 'I know this is presumptuous of me, ma'am, but if Mr Robbins is not in attendance at the moment, I would deem it an honour if you would be my companion at the ball tonight. It sounds fun and I suspect you may be in the same boat as myself. Namely, a stranger in town with time to kill until the stage leaves tomorrow.'

'Mr Robbins is not in attendance at the moment because he's dead,' she said gravely, and pushed open the door into the hotel. That might the explain the world-weariness in the otherwise beautiful eyes.

'My apologies, ma'am,' he said, following her. 'The suggestion was out of place and its delivery clumsy.'

Part way across the lobby she stopped, turned and appraised him carefully up and down. 'There I go again. Yes, it does sound a pleasant way to while away some time. What time shall we meet?'

'I think the poster said eight. So, say that time here in the lobby?'

'Fine.'

He accompanied her upstairs.

142

'I look forward to the evening, Mr Edson,' she said, as they parted and she headed for her room.

He needed a break such as would be provided by the ball but he was loath to leave the bag of loot unattended. He went downstairs to the reception desk. 'When are the rooms cleaned?'

'Every morning from ten onwards, or by arrangement if you prefer,' the clerk said.

'And when are the commodes emptied?'

'As and when required, sir. Why? Does the gentleman require it to emptied now?'

'No, no. It's just that I need my rest and don't want to be disturbed.'

'I'll make a note of your request now, sir.' He scribbled the room number in a book with 'Not to be disturbed unless requested' against it. 'There you are, sir. There's also a "Do not disturb" sign in your room. Just slip that over the doorknob as a reminder.'

'And finally, I could do with some reading matter while I'm resting. Can you tell me where in town I can buy a newspaper?'

'I can save your legs, sir,' the man said, bending down and extracting a paper from the shelf underneath. 'That's today's Denver newsheet. We've finished with it. It's all yours.'

'That's very thoughtful. And thank you very much.'

'Anything to oblige, sir. That's what we're here for.'

Returning upstairs, he identified which was the cleaning cupboard in the corridor and checked its interior. Then, back in his room, he took the porcelain pot out of the commode and deposited it under paraphernalia in the cleaning cabinet in the passageway. He inserted the moneybag into the now vacant commode. It was a tight fit but he could just do it. He opened out the newspaper and used it to cover the bag, tucking the paper neatly around all its sides completely masking it; and he closed the commode lid.

He met his partner for the evening in the lobby. 'You look radiant, ma'am,' he said by way of greeting.

'Thank you,' she replied, 'And you look even more handsome, sir.'

She took his arm. 'Please call me Portia.'

'Very well, Portia,' he said, 'on the condition you call me Tom.'

Then, along paved sidewalks bathed in the luxury of the latest development in public lighting, he escorted her to the appointed location.

What must have been a bare, ugly meeting room by day had been transformed by red-white-and-blue bunting and flags. Ribbons looped in festoons over windows and walls. Below the decorations the scene was set off by the ladies in their laces, frocks and frills. More austere, most of the men were dark-suited while here and there could be seen a soldier's uniform.

On a raised platform a band played a medley of patriotic tunes.

Ellis charted a course between guests and potted plants, guiding his companion to the punchbowl.

'I always feel naked at these things without a glass in my hand,' he said.

'What a splendid occasion,' she said, when they had full glasses and stood aside to view the gathering.

The evening progressed in that way with polite conversation until the band was replaced by musicians with fiddles playing music for dancing.

'Are you familiar with the waltz, Mr Edson?' she asked, when she recognized the rhythm.

'It will be my pleasure.'

They continued in such a fashion, enjoying the occasion and each other's company. Not wishing to see her eyes cloud as he had seen previously, he asked no questions about her husband or related matters. Likewise she asked him no personal questions.

Finally, around ten she stifled a yawn. 'I don't wish to appear rude but I really must retire. You may feel the same. We both have another long day of travelling before us.'

'Of course.'

Some five minutes later, she paused in the passageway before the door to her room in the hotel.

'It's been a wonderful evening and you have been a charming escort, Mr Edson.' He shook her hand and bowed slightly.

'My pleasure, ma'am.'

'Then I will wish you goodnight, Tom.'

'Goodnight, Portia.'

She glanced back as she turned the key in the lock. 'Oh, maybe you can help me with my trunk tomorrow?'

'Of course.'

And he returned to his room, checked that his hidden bundle was still intact, then went to sleep, his gun close by.

FOURTEEN

'Oh, Ellis,' Ann Scarpelli said, as she stepped down from the stage on to the Denver boardwalk. 'I've missed you so much.'

'Hush,' he whispered, pulling her close. 'I'm known as Tom Edson here.' He took her baggage from the driver and guided her by the arm to the hotel.

'We've only got an hour before the stage leaves,' he said in the lobby, 'and I've got things to tell you.'

Mrs Robbins was coming down the stairs as they ascended. 'Don't forget my trunk, Tom,' she said as they passed.

'No, Portia, 1 won't,' he said with a polite smile.

Ann threw a quizzical glance back at the receding bustle that decorated the swinging hips. 'Who's that?'

'Just a woman who's travelling on the same coach as us.'

'How do you know her?'

'We met yesterday at the ticket office. Spent a little time chatting last evening. That's all.' He smiled at the concern on her face. 'Quite innocent. Just socializing. No bed or anything like that.'

He showed her to his room.

'Now about Frank,' he began to say, as he closed the door behind them, but she interrupted him.

'I heard that bodies have been found in some burned-out cabin. They say that the bodies were burned beyond recognition, but I've been hoping and praying that one of them was Frank.'

As she spoke the last words his face took on a serious aspect. He turned to face her and leant against the door. 'One was.'

'Well, what could be better? Why are you looking so glum?'

'Ann, he didn't die in the fire; I shot him.'

She shrugged, her face showing no emotion. 'So.'

'Well, I hadn't intended to. But he pulled a gun and it was either him or me.'

'Why did he threaten you with a gun?'

'It was over you. He identified the cigarette case. I was clumsy.'

She laughed. 'Over me? Makes me feel important. My! I have the power over life or death – like in some melodrama or Greek tragedy.'

'It's not a laughing matter, either that your husband is dead – or that I was the cause.'

'Ellis, what's got into you?'

He dropped on to the bed and stared at the floor.

'Well?' she pressed.

'Something's just hit me,' he said eventually. 'You and me – it's not going to work.'

Given the robbery and intensity of events since he had not had much time to think about his relationship with Mrs Scarpelli. The thing had just rolled on, ·unquestioned. Vaguely in the background, unpleasant aspects of her character had been floating disconnectedly in his mind – but suddenly, face to face with her in the hotel room, seeing the hardness in her eyes, things were clicking into place.

He let out a deep, conclusive sigh. 'I've decided. I'm not taking you with me.'

'What?'

'The notion of us, our relationship, it just smells funny. In fact, the more I think about it, it's dead before it starts.'

She softened. 'Oh, Ellis.' And she tried to nestle against his chest.

But when he thrust her away, a greater hardness came to her eyes. 'It's that woman, isn't it?' she challenged. 'You've got another woman. It's that Portia woman. That's it. Just because she's younger than me.'

'No. I hardly know the girl.'

'Then why?'

'Something to do with the cold light of day.'

She thought in it, then concluded, 'You never intended taking me.'

He looked at the accusing face. Now she was beginning to annoy him. 'Don't be stupid, woman. Why did you think I've arranged to see you here, and waited for you?'

'Then why are we not leaving together?'

'It's just occurred to me. When you wanted Frank out of the way all I could think of was that was my good fortune. Your perfume, your body, everything about you, all fazed me. Ann, I killed him, not to get him out of the way but simply because he was throwing lead at me. It was the only way I could stop him. When he was lying gut-shot on the floor back there in that cabin, I thought that's stopped him putting holes in me but it's also solved another problem. The way was clear for me and you. But I hadn't planned it like that, it just fell that way. And that's the way I've felt until we just met up again. But when I told you about his demise, you showed no emotion. None at all. That hit me like a hammer blow.

You've got a cold side. You must have loved him once, romped in the sack and all the other stuff that a loving couple do, the kind of things we've done over a couple of days. Yet his death meant nothing to you. A leopard doesn't change its spots – whether it's male or female. I see now, the way your feelings changed to him, they could just as easily change towards me somewhere along the way. Frank said he guessed there'd been a line of fellers going through your bed. I paid his words no heed at the time. But now, I believe him.'

'It's not true.'

He looked at her face, noted the increasing animosity building up in her eyes.

'They say absence makes the heart grow fonder,' he said, 'but—'

'They also say out of sight out of mind,' she snapped.

He stood up. 'So, no malice, baby. I just don't see the two of us setting up home together. It was something short and sweet while it lasted. But it's finished.'

Brill was no regular horseman, plus the horse underneath him was still new to him. As a consequence he was unable to get the maximum speed from the animal. Nevertheless over the many miles from Lauderburg he had managed to reduce the distance between himself and the coach.

When he eventually caught sight of Denver from afar, he was amazed at its scale. Once into the main street, he had some trouble controlling his horse among the thronging traffic which was unfamiliar to both of them.

Thus he was glad when, at the end of the busy thoroughfare, he could see the object of his pursuit, the lurching Concord coach, being circled for its return trip.

He dismounted and took the opportunity to calm his horse while he watched liverymen manoeuvre the team into completing the turn-around.

When the driver finally hauled on the brake at the depot, he went over.

'Excuse me, pal,' he said, thumbing his badge. 'When you came in, there was a woman aboard.'

'There were several.'

Although Brill was not closely acquainted with the woman, he had seen her about town on many occasions and could describe her.

'Yeah, I remember her,' the man said.

'Did you see where she went?'

The man ruminated on his tobacco cud and ejected a stream of juice into the ground. 'She was met by a guy.' He pointed. 'They went into the hotel yonder.'

'Thanks.'

Brill pulled on the horse's bridle to swing the

animal round, and he headed in the indicated direction.

'You bastard,' Ann snarled.

'Now that isn't ladylike language, my dear,' Ellis countered. 'And it demonstrates the different side of you that's comes out when the chips are down.'

'No man dumps me,' she hissed between gritted teeth.

'This one is. Don't worry, woman, I'll give you your cut. With all the other guys kicking up the daisies, it'll be a clear twenty grand.'

She flew at him with raised fingers, talons ready to scratch at his flesh. He gripped her wrists and easily prevented the attack. Then he flung her so that she slumped into a chair.

'You can't leave me as easy as that.'

'Can and will.'

'You'll regret it.'

'Huh, what can you do?'

'With that massacre back at the stage, the hunt for you is going to be wide-ranging. You're forgetting, Ellis Pearce, I know your name and where you'll be hiding out.'

He laughed. 'I told you that wasn't my given name. What do you take me for, a greenhorn in these matters? My folks were Russian settlers and they burdened me with something which even a

person of your education would find unpro-
nounceable. Hell, woman, Ellis Pearce is just one
of my many travelling names.'

'Think you're smart, don't you? But I still know
you'll be holing up in Nome.'

Yes, Ellis thought, he regretted that one slip.
He made it a rule in all his operations never to
divulge any personal data. But the way things had
been going with Ann at first, thinking they were
heading for something permanent together, his
guard had been temporarily down. But it was not
an important slip.

'You exude an air of refinement and education,
ma'am, but you don't know much about history
or geography. Alaska was originally part of Russia.
That's how come my folks were there. Anybody
who goes out there looking for somebody with a
Russian name is going to have a problem. Most of
the population have got a framed picture of the
Tsar hanging on the wall!'

He eyed her as she sat seething in frustration.
'Now act sensibly, woman. You're going to get half
the total. Now that there are no more claimants,
that works out at twenty grand. You can buy any
number of gigolos with that.'

The jibe was enough to cause her to fly at him
again but he'd had enough and this time he
clipped her smartly across the jaw. In his time in
the snowlands he'd tussled with mountain-men

and burly trappers. Thus his blow to a woman's jaw was enough to lay her out. He looked down at her still form. 'They say hell hath no fury like a woman scorned. OK, I can put up with that.'

And he set about splitting the money and preparing to leave.

Brill heavy-footed into the lobby.

'Woman and a feller came in short while back,' he said, thumbing his badge. 'Who are they?'

'Don't know the lady,' the clerk at the counter replied. 'She just came in on the stage from Mortimer. The gentleman is Mr Edson, one of our guests.'

'He Canadian?'

The man thought. 'I wondered about that. The way he rolled his r's. Thought maybe he was Scotch. But you're right, come to think of it. Canadian.'

'What room is he in?'

The clerk looked at the book. 'Room Five, second floor.' Then added, 'But he'll be down shortly. He's catching the noon stage to Cheyenne.' He noted the gun coming from the holster. 'Oh dear, is this something to do with the trouble?'

'What trouble?'

'There's been lots of banging and shouting coming from that room for the last few minutes.'

'Don't get concerned if you hear some more. And you keep quiet.'

Upstairs, he walked lightly along the carpeted passageway and located Room Five. Noises of movement came from within. He continued to the end where there was a turning that led to other rooms. He took up position out of sight and waited, gun ready.

Eventually the door opened and a man stepped out carrying a large carpetbag. His back was to Brill as he made to close the door.

Brill stepped clear. 'Oh, Mr Pearce?' he said, in a light questioning tone.

'Yes,' the man said, turning. He saw the badge and gun and realized his unthinking mistake.

He forced a quizzical expression. 'I'm afraid you're in error, young man.' He tightened his grip on the bag. 'And why the gun may I ask? What is this?'

The words were formed with a softness unfamiliar to Brill's ears. Whether or not it was Canadian intonation, he didn't know. But he did know this was his man.

'I've got some handcuffs here, mister. Put down the bag and turn round with your hands behind you. And—'

Before his challenger could make any more stipulations, Ellis swung up the bag and hurled it at his questioner in one fluid movement, knocking aside the gun.

As Brill fell to the floor under the weight, Ellis wrenched open his jacket to yank out his own gun. The first bullet thudded into the bag. The second never left the barrel. There was an explosion and he staggered against the wall.

His gun arm hung slack, the shoulder above it shattered.

He raised his head clumsily to see the woman standing in the doorway, a smoking pocket-pistol in her hand.

The pain expressed in his face did not prevent a sardonic smile coming to his lips.

'You know, sometimes being a lady is more important than being a woman.'

As his free hand groped towards the wound, there was another loud report and a bloody crater appeared in his forehead. He swung in an arc against the wall leaving a long, bloody smear on the expensive wallpaper and fell to the floor.

Mrs Scarpelli turned the gun towards Brill.

'That's no use, ma'am. I heard the hammer click on an empty chamber.'

He crossed over to her and took the gun. He hefted the gun before slipping it into his pocket. 'Derringer, two shots. And you've had both.'

Her eyes were still directed at the body, her brain slowly absorbing what she had done. 'He was leaving me.' She looked up, her mind returning to practicalities. 'You ... you're the new deputy at Lauderburg.'

'Not for much longer, ma'am.' He picked up the bag and gestured for her to go back in the room.

'What are you going to do with me?' she asked.

'I'm taking you in, ma'am. As my last job in the post of temporary peace officer.'

He dumped the bag on the bed and opened it.

'The other half is in my valise,' she said.

She watched him check the contents of the second bag. 'Listen, when I shot him out there, I saved your life. That must mean something to you. There's a lot of money there. Let me go and give me a cut. Nobody'll question a little missing, Travelling money, just enough to get me some distance.'

'Ain't mine to give, ma'am.'

He closed the valise. 'Get your things and let's move.'

'Well, at least give me a chance,' she said. 'Let me go. Surely saving your life deserves something?'

'Ma'am, I ain't falling into the error of attaching myself too much to the viewpoint of someone who, for their own purposes, has incidentally saved me from a bullet. That's not why you shot him out there and you darn well knows it.'

'Please,' she whimpered.

'No point in trying that feminine stuff either, Mrs Scarpelli. You're a hard, calculating woman and no mistake. It was your pal out there in the corridor who led the gang that killed Florida Jones and the others, but *you* masterminded the operation. The way I sees things, if you hadn't planned it, my old buddy Florida would still be alive today. That's almost as good as pulling the trigger yourself. So plead all you like, ma'am, I'm still taking you in.'

There was an increasing commotion outside and the door suddenly opened.

Amongst the jabber Brill heard some woman say, 'Dear me. Such a gentleman too. I was only dancing with him last night.'

A man nosed in, wielding a gun. 'What the hell's happening here?'

Brill saw the shiny shield of a local lawman and pointed to his own badge.

'I'd like to get the money into a Denver bank,' he said, after he'd explained events. 'It's my experience of late that stagecoaches can be a mite vulnerable. And I'd like you to hold the lady in your cell until I've cleared up things here and arranged travel back to Lauderburg.'

After the paperwork had been completed and passage fixed, Brill came to collect his prisoner.

'I've been doing some thinking,' he whispered

as the two stood on the sidewalk waiting for other passengers to board. 'I'll tell you what I'm willing to do. Despite the fact it wasn't your intention to save my skin, it surely is a fact you did stop your pal dropping me. So in court I won't make mention of whatever argument you had against him or that he was ditching you and skedaddling. I'll just say you shot him while he was levelling up on me, which is the truth, the bare truth, but the truth nonetheless. What you tell the court about your reasoning for doing so is up to you and I won't argue with it. I figure that's what you in your high-falutin' world would call a *quid pro quo*. They might take that into account when fixing your sentence. Who knows? Turn on the charm, flutter those eyelids and the jury might see things your way.'

She said nothing, finally realizing that that was the best she could expect.

He gave support to her arm in preparation to board. 'And as a bonus,' he added, 'to show how understanding I am, if you don't give me any trouble on the way back to Lauderburg I won't put any handcuffs on those refined, dainty wrists.'